OTHER BOOKS BY BRENDA SEABROOKE

The Vampire in My Bathtub
The Care and Feeding of Dragons
Under the Pear Tree
The Swan's Gift
Looking for Diamonds
The Haunting of Holroyd Hill
The Bridges of Summer
The Dragon That Ate Summer
The Chester Town Tea Party
Judy Scuppernong
The Boy Who Saved the Town
Jerry on the Line
Home Is Where They Take You In
The Best Burglar Alarm

THE HAUNTING AT STRATTON FALLS

THE

HAUNTING

at

STRATTON FALLS

Brenda Seabrooke

DUTTON CHILDREN'S BOOKS ● NEW YORK

Copyright © 2000 by Brenda Seabrooke

Library of Congress Cataloging-in-Publication Data
Seabrooke, Brenda.
The haunting at Stratton Falls / by Brenda Seabrooke.—1st ed.
p. cm.
Summary: At Christmastime in 1944, while staying with disagreeable cousins in New York State because her father is in Europe fighting in World War II, eleven-year-old Abby discovers that her relatives' old house is haunted by the ghost of a girl from the Civil War era.
ISBN 0-525-46389-5
[1. Ghosts—Fiction. 2. Christmas—Fiction. 3. Cousins—Fiction. 4. World War, 1939–1945—United States—Fiction. 5. New York (State)—Fiction.] I. Title.
PZ7.S4376 Has 2000 [Fic]—dc21 99-089892

Published in the United States by Dutton Children's Books,
a division of Penguin Putnam Books for Young Readers
345 Hudson Street, New York, New York 10014
www.penguinputnam.com

Designed by Amy Berniker
Printed in USA   First Edition
10 9 8 7 6 5 4 3 2 1

For *KEVIN*, the snow aficionado,

and *KERRIA*, the creator of dollhouses

THE HAUNTING AT STRATTON FALLS

*T*he elm tree loomed above Abby, its leafless branches high above the bank of the icy Stratton River. "All the way to Canada? You can see another country from up there?" She touched the rough bark of the tree as if it were magic.

Chad glanced at Ginny and Nancy and grinned. "Sure. You can see over the treetops clear to Canada." He pointed across at the trees above the falls.

Abby hadn't climbed many trees, just a few live oaks with low, widespread limbs. In Jacksonville, where she had always lived, the trees were mostly palms or oaks. She had never seen another country, so she swung herself up. "It just looks like the other side of the river," she said from the lowest limb.

"You have to go higher," Chad said.

Abby went up, not letting go of a limb until she had a handhold on the next one. Now she could see a blue haze in the distance above the treetops. "Is that Canada?"

"No, keep going."

Abby climbed higher. "How will I know when I see it?"

"You'll know," Chad said. "It'll look like the farthest place in the world."

Ginny giggled. Abby glanced down, and her stomach swooped. Chad, Ginny, and Nancy looked so small. The ground seemed like the farthest place now. She must have climbed halfway up the tree. A sudden gust of wind rocked the branches. Abby grabbed the trunk. Her foot slipped into a V between trunk and branch. She tried to pull free, but her oxford wedged firmly.

"Did you see Canada yet?" Chad yelled as Ginny and Nancy giggled.

"I don't know." Abby hugged the trunk as its branches swayed. "I'm stuck. I can't get down."

"That's silly," Nancy said. "Nobody gets stuck in a tree."

"Come on down," Chad said. "We haven't got all day."

Tears started in Abby's eyes, but she was afraid to let go to wipe them as the wind whipped around her. "I can't."

"Don't be such a baby," Chad said. "Scaredy-cat!" Then he laughed and chanted "Scaredy-cat, 'fraidy-cat!" as they ran away, toward Nancy's house, leaving Abby alone in the tree.

"Come back!" Abby called, but they didn't seem to hear. The wind blew harder, stinging her cheeks. The tree groaned as its branches tossed and heaved like a wild horse until she thought she couldn't hold on a minute longer. Then it paused.

Abby shivered and clutched the trunk and tried to jerk her foot free, but the shoe wouldn't budge. Her palms were clammy as she surveyed her situation. It was late afternoon, but she was stuck here until dark. The grown-ups would miss her then, and Chad would have to tell them where she was and they would rescue her. But Abby didn't want to stay in the tree that long. She was cold and scared. She would have to free herself somehow. She tried to analyze the situation the way her dad had taught her. She could hear him saying, "There are almost always at least two ways of looking at something, Abby. Go over the information that you have and look for ways to change things."

My foot is stuck in the tree. If I jerk it too hard, I

might fall. The wind is blowing and I'm cold. It's a long time until dark.

She stopped. Analyzing was only making her feel worse. Maybe she was doing it wrong. She tried again. I'm stuck in the tree because my shoe is caught. Wait. That was it, the solution. Her shoe was caught, not her foot. If she unlaced her shoe, maybe she could slip her foot out.

As Abby let go of the trunk, the wind sprang into action again. Between gusts she reached with her right hand to untie the laces of her left shoe. That was the easy part. Slowly, she slid her foot out of the oxford, but as soon as her foot was free, the shoe tipped over and fell into the river below.

"Oh no, my shoe!" Abby scrambled down after it but the shoe had disappeared, leaving a star-shaped hole in the ice near the bank. She stuck a branch into the hole to drag for her shoe. She snagged a rusty can and some muddy leaves but couldn't find her shoe. Maybe the current under the ice had already carried it over Stratton Falls.

Abby dreaded telling her mother and making her worry. They had used up their war ration coupons to buy warm clothes when they moved from Florida to upstate New York to live with her mother's brother and his family. Now after only a week she had lost her shoe. How would she get another?

Her mother had been having terrible migraine headaches since the telegram that reported Abby's father was missing in the war in Europe. Abby would never forget that afternoon. It was Halloween, and she was in her witch costume, ready to go trick-or-treating, when the doorbell rang. The Western Union messenger handed her mother a telegram that said he had been missing since September 30. The headaches started after that. Sometimes her mother was sick for days, lying in a darkened room with an ice bag on her head.

Her father had gone overseas with the army in the spring of 1944, after training in Texas. Now he was missing, and they'd had to move up to this strange cold place where Abby felt left out of everything. And Chad made things worse. He made fun of her when she didn't know things, like what blancmange pudding was or when she thought Parcheesi was something to eat.

The ground was knobby under her stockinged foot. And cold. Something fell on her eyelashes and her eyes blurred as she hurried up the hill. Light spilled into the gathering dusk from the windows of the big gray stone house at the top of the hill. Bits of white stuff splatted against her eyes, on her nose, her mouth. Little white dots fell around her from the darkening sky. Snow! Abby stuck out her tongue and tasted her first snowflake. She ran to the house with the news, but everybody looked instead at her stockinged foot.

"Abby, where's your shoe?" Polly asked, bouncing her blonde pigtails.

"Did you lose it?" Patty asked, bouncing hers, too.

Abby's mother pulled her blue cardigan close and rubbed the back of her neck below her light brown hair. "Oh, Abby," Mrs. Sanders said with a sigh, a tiny frown above her blue eyes, "now you only have your dress-up shoes."

"It's all right, Ellen. We'll think of something," Aunt Noreen said, touching her sister-in-law's shoulder. She sent Abby for her house slippers.

When Uncle Thomas came home, he said not to worry. He was a doctor, and his patients gave him ration coupons they didn't need. He was sure he had one for a pair of shoes.

As they sat around the table after supper, Aunt Noreen said, "Abby, I don't understand why you were in the tree."

"I wanted to see Canada," Abby explained.

"You can't see Canada from here," Uncle Thomas said. "Not even from a tree. Chad, did you have anything to do with this?"

Chad shot Abby a dagger look. "You might see Canada if you look real hard," he mumbled.

Uncle Thomas made Chad apologize for tricking Abby. But she was miserable, as if she were in trouble instead of Chad. Now he would never like her.

As they cleared the table her mother went upstairs to rest. "I don't have a headache," she assured Abby with a smile. "I'm just a little tired."

But Abby felt guilty. Her mother was tired from worrying about the lost shoe. She jumped up to help Aunt Noreen with the dishes, scraping plates and stacking them beside the kitchen sink. "I can wash," she said.

"Why, thank you, Abby. I haven't had any help since Margie quit working for me to join the WAVEs. Chad and the twins can help, too."

Chad refused to wash and the twins were too small to reach the cabinets and sink, so Abby washed, Polly and Patty dried, and Chad put the dishes away. Abby thought he got the easiest job, but he scowled fiercely under the dark hair that fell over his eyes and said, "This is woman's work." Now she had made Chad hate her even more.

She couldn't seem to do anything right. McNab, Chad's black Scottie, growled at Abby when she picked up his dishes to wash last. "I'm not taking anything away from you," she told him as she set a clean bowl of water on the floor. He curled his lip at her. He didn't seem to like her either.

Chad stomped off to his room. He was twelve, only a year older than Abby, but he acted so superior, just like Nancy Hughes. Ginny Gray acted that way, too, even though she and Abby were the same age. The twins didn't, but they were only six. Abby counted up; four people liked her and three didn't. And a dog. But those were the three she wanted to play with.

Abby wrung out the dishcloth and hung it to dry. In the parlor the twins played checkers while Aunt Noreen read a magazine. Abby settled on the window seat and opened her book, *Ivanhoe,* about lords and ladies a long time ago. When the twins went to bed, Aunt Noreen went upstairs, too. "Turn off the lights when you come up," she said. "Uncle Thomas will be out late on a house call."

Abby noticed the silence first. The house was hardly ever quiet with seven people and one crabby dog in it, but now the silence seemed to wrap itself around her. She had trouble concentrating on the characters, knights battling with swords. Abby hated war, even the long-ago kind to rescue ladies in castles. Her dad had been fighting Nazis somewhere in Europe when he went missing. Now they didn't know where he was or even if he was alive. The telegram said Holland, but he could be in France or Belgium or a place called Luxembourg. His unit might even have reached Germany. Why did people have to fight wars, anyway? It was all so awful. Abby hadn't seen him now in more than a year. Sometimes she looked in the mirror and wondered if she had changed so much he wouldn't know her when he came home. The words on the page of her book seemed to dissolve as tears burned Abby's eyes. Quickly, she blinked them away.

She wouldn't cry. She turned off the lamp and pulled the heavy black curtains back from the window. The world outside had changed. Snow fell like thick lace, covering the lawn. Snow shrouded the bushes and evergreen trees, outlined the skeletal limbs of bare trees, and erased the front walk. Abby leaned against the cushions in the window seat and watched the falling snow. For a whiie she forgot about her mother's headaches, her missing father, her homesickness for Florida, Chad's meanness, McNab's crabbiness. For a while she thought of nothing but the hypnotic, falling snow.

Abby jumped when the grandfather clock in the hall boomed eleven times. She closed the curtains and went to the kitchen for a glass of milk.

On the way back, Abby crossed the hall to the stairs. A trail of wet footprints led across the slate floor from the front door to the parlor. Somebody must have gone out and come back in without her hearing. It couldn't have been Uncle Thomas. He would have used the back entrance from the garage. Abby measured with her foot. The prints were only a little smaller than her foot.

Could it have been Nancy or Ginny? Or one of the twins wearing somebody else's shoes? Whoever it was hadn't made any noise. She didn't see how anybody could have been that quiet. But when she looked in the parlor, no one was there.

TWO

*A*bby pulled red rubber boots on over two pairs of socks. She had never worn boots in Jacksonville, not even rain boots. She hated wearing Chad's outgrown ones. Abby was lucky to get them because rubber was being made into tires for jeeps and trucks. She had helped collect used rubber and scrap metal and old newspapers back home, but she still wished she had anybody's boots but Chad's. Most of her outdoor clothes were his hand-me-downs, too, but everybody had to help the war effort. She could wear old clothes.

The boots were scuffed and stained, and the gray jacket and navy pants had been ripped and mended several times. Abby liked her hat. Aunt Noreen had knitted it out of yarn from an old sweater. It was red, her favorite color. She wound a long navy wool scarf of Uncle Thomas's around her neck.

She zipped up the jacket and went out the front door to play in snow for the first time in her life. Her feet made slapping sounds in the rubber boots.

"Hey, Abby!"

She turned around.

"Bombs away!" Chad shouted. *Splat.* A snowball hit the middle of her face. Snow went up her nose.

Splat. Snowballs hit her again, in the nose, mouth, both eyes, her chin. Her lashes were frosted with snow. She turned her back, but snowballs continued to hit her with machine-gun regularity.

"Stop it!" she yelled at Chad.

But he didn't stop. As Abby leaned over to make a snowball, a hard one hit her squarely in the back, knocking her facedown in the snow. She struggled to her feet, a barrage of snowballs raining over her. Snow migrated down her neck, up her sleeves, into her boots and mittens. She managed to make a small lumpy snowball and lob it at Chad, but it missed and he let fly with another fusillade. Where did he get so many? He must have been making snowballs for hours, stockpiling them to ambush her.

When he finally ran out of ammunition, Abby went back into the house. "Crybaby," Chad taunted. She wasn't crying. Her tears were caused by the cold, sting-ing snow.

Chunks of snow fell from her clothes as she hurried through the house. She hung her snow clothes on the wall pegs in the back hall and sat on the bottom stair to take off the boots. Snow puddled on the stone floor as she upended the boots on the rack. She put on her house slippers and settled in the parlor window seat to rethink her ideas about snow. It was not soft and fluffy. It was hard and cold and hurtful.

Polly and Patty brought their cards and asked her to play a game of old maid with them.

"It's more fun with you than Chad," Polly confided.

"He always wins," Patty added.

Abby loved the twins. They were so sweet, not at all like their half brother.

Chad wasn't really Abby's cousin. His father had died a month after he was born, and his mother had married Uncle Thomas a year later. On the long train trip north, she had imagined what fun she would have with all her cousins. But it hadn't worked out that way. Chad played with Nancy and Ginny, and when she joined in, he ran her off with his teasing and tricks. She played with the twins, but they liked to make up games nobody else could understand and Abby was often left to herself.

After three games of old maid, they decided to play one of their games, Ragamatoofin. They went to their room to get the board and didn't come back.

Abby found her place in *Ivanhoe* and curled up in the window seat to read, but her eyes strayed to the scene outside. Chad and Nancy and Ginny were making a snowman. Chad made stick arms. Nancy made buttons from bits of coal. Ginny made a face out of coal. Chad covered the head with coal hair. The hair went down on each side like pigtails. Abby touched her own dark pigtails tied with blue plaid bows. Then Chad stuck a red yarn bow on the end of each pigtail and they all laughed. Suddenly Abby recognized herself. They had made a snowman to look like her, a snowAbby.

"Abby, why aren't you out playing in the snow?" her mother said from the doorway.

"I was cold," Abby said.

"Then I'm glad you came in," she said, smiling. "You're not used to this climate yet. You don't want to catch cold."

"I won't," Abby said. She didn't want her mother to have that to worry about, too. When you had a big worry that you couldn't do anything about, like her father being missing, little worries seemed to multiply and get bigger.

Abby tried to concentrate on her book when her mother went to the kitchen, but she couldn't. Her daddy had grown up in Florida, too. Abby had read about Europe in the encyclopedia at school. A lot of snow fell there in winter. Her dad was seeing his first snow, too. That meant he was fighting two enemies, the Nazis and the snow. In Holland the canals froze over and people skated on them as if they were streets. There was sure to be a lot of snow. She hoped he had warm boots and clothes.

The door to the kitchen slammed. Chad! Abby moved to the sofa with her book. She wouldn't let him know she had seen that awful snowAbby outside the window.

"Where are the twins?" he asked.

"Playing Ragamatoofin in their room."

He grinned. "They'll be busy for hours." He got a box out of the hall closet and took out the matchstick house he was making for them. "Tell me if you hear them coming."

Abby nodded. She didn't think he could finish it in time for Christmas. He was only halfway to the roof and didn't have enough matchsticks. He chopped off the head of a used wooden kitchen match and glued it in place. He acted as if nothing had happened. Suddenly Abby was furious. "Why did you pelt me with all those snowballs?"

As he glanced up his brown eyes glinted almost red in the firelight. "Because it's fun. You looked so funny all bent over in a lump." He grinned, sticking his front teeth over his bottom lip. He looked like a goat.

It was the grin that did it. Suddenly Abby hated him. "Fun!" she burst out. "Why is it fun to throw snow in another person's face so she can't see and can hardly breathe?"

He shrugged and decapitated another match. "It just is."

Abby threw her book at him. She missed and hit the house. Matchsticks cracked and broke and fell off. Chad looked down at the mess in surprise, as though he couldn't believe that anybody would wreck his house. "You broke the house. What'd you do that for?"

"Because I'm angry at you." Abby hadn't meant to break the house. But it served him right.

"Why?"

"For throwing all those snowballs at me. They hurt."

"You could have thrown them back at me."

"I couldn't. I don't know how to make a snowball. I've never seen snow before in my whole life. I thought snow would be fun. And you spoiled it all."

"But you broke the house. Now I'll never get it finished by Christmas."

Abby wasn't sorry. "Too bad. You threw snowballs at me and I threw a book at you. So we're even."

"No, we're not. I didn't break anything of yours."

"Yes, you did."

"What? What did I break?"

Abby thought for a minute. "You broke my dream of snow."

"That's stupid. You can't break a dream."

"Yes, you can." He'd also broken her dream of fun with her cousins, but she didn't want him to know about that.

Aunt Noreen interrupted the argument. "Stop this instantly. Ellen hasn't had a migraine since you came up here. I don't want you two to cause one."

"We weren't doing anything," Chad protested.

"You were arguing."

"But—"

"No buts, Chad. If you can't play quietly, you can go to your room." She went back to the kitchen.

"See what you did."

"What *I* did?" Abby glared at him.

He didn't reply but began to pick up the bits of the house. This was the time to ask him, when he was off guard, before he had time to think up something. "Why did Nancy or Ginny come over here last night?"

"Huh? What do you mean?" His surprise seemed genuine.

"One of them came over here last night."

"They didn't."

"I *saw* the footprints. What are you up to?"

"Nothing. I don't know what you are talking about."
He took the box upstairs.

Abby sat in the parlor watching the light fade through the window until it was time to pull the curtains and turn on the lamps. If the footprints weren't Nancy's or Ginny's, whose were they?

THREE

Snow was the main topic of conversation at supper, how deep it was, how heavy, how wet, how beautiful, how great for sledding. Abby waited for someone to mention the snowAbby, but by the time Aunt Noreen served the stewed peaches for dessert no one had. Maybe they all thought it was just an ordinary snowman.

But Abby knew it wasn't. And so did Chad with his sly grins. She schemed as she passed bowls and platters and didn't look at him, even though he kept asking her for beans and potatoes and gravy and corn and biscuits. She noticed that he only took a little of everything she passed to him the second time. He was just being a pest again. But she would fix him. She had a plan.

Abby ignored Chad as they washed and put away

the dishes after supper, even when he brought back a cup, a plate, and a fork and told her she hadn't washed them thoroughly. She knew she had. He was putting bits of food he got out of the garbage on the clean dishes, a smear of gravy, a smashed bean, a dab of potato. She didn't say anything. She scraped another plate into the garbage and then moved the can closer to the sink so she could keep her eye on it as she washed.

Chad stopped putting food on the clean dishes then. She wanted to make a face at him so he would know she was on to him, but that might make him suspicious. She concentrated on the soapy sink as he put away the last pot and went to his room. Abby wiped the sink with the dishcloth. The grown-ups were listening to the radio in the parlor. She didn't want to hear the scary war news. She had her own war right here in Stratton Falls, New York. She went up to her room to wait until time to go on her raid.

The Lamberts' house was like a castle to Abby. And old. Uncle Thomas said it was built in 1840. Her Florida house was an airy, salmon-colored, six-room house with a wraparound porch, all on one floor. This house seemed dark, but maybe that was because the days were shorter in upstate New York. Colder, too, but maybe that was because it had so many rooms. Downstairs on the right of a long hall were Uncle Thomas's study, the front stairway, and the parlor. On the other side, a cloakroom had been made into a bathroom and closet. Beyond it was the dining room, kitchen, and back hall with the servants' stairway. Abby's room, with its dark ornate Victorian furniture, was over the study. It was gloomy despite the cheery pink-flowered quilt Aunt Noreen had put on the bed. The stairway, bathroom, Uncle Thomas and Aunt Noreen's room, and the sewing room were on the same side. Across the hall was her mother's room, then Chad's, the twins' room, and the back stairs.

At ten-forty-five the snow outside made the night almost as bright as day. Surely everyone was asleep by now, Abby thought as she went down the back stairs to the hall. She slipped snow clothes over her pajamas, pulled on her boots, and eased open the back door. The snow looked blue now under a darker blue sky. The roofs of the house, garage, and barn were piled with soft snow. The river at the foot of the hill was iced over almost all the way across. Abby bet the falls were almost frozen, too. It was cold enough. She was glad the wind wasn't blowing.

She went around the house to the front and paused to check the windows. Not a speck of light showed through the blackout curtains. Aunt Noreen had made sure of that. The war news must be bad. Abby had heard the grown-ups talking in whispers about the Nazi breakout in the Battle of the Bulge, but she didn't think the Nazis could come here. They were too far upstate for the Nazis to bomb them, and why would they want to anyway? Stratton Falls didn't have any shipyards or factories. It was a small town in the middle of farmland in the Stratton River Valley.

When the war news was good, Aunt Noreen didn't black out the windows until full dark, and sometimes she forgot a crack here or there. But when the news was bad, she did it early. Today she had pulled the curtains across the windows at four. Aunt Noreen's windows wouldn't guide any enemy bombers.

Abby was glad for the blackout. It meant that nobody would see her from the house unless they opened the curtains. Nancy's and Ginny's houses were too far away.

The snowAbby with its ugly stick arms and coal features stood like an icy sculpture in front of the house. Abby worked quickly, removing the pigtails, dropping the unneeded bits of coal, as if they had fallen off into the surrounding snow. She finished her work and hurried around the house to the back door. She struggled out of her snow things. Her boots were wet, but the jacket and pants were dry as she hung them in the back hall, so if Chad checked them they wouldn't give her away.

She put her slippers on and tiptoed through the kitchen to the front stairs, which were closer to her bedroom. Abby turned on the hall light and glanced at the door. Wet tracks gleamed on the floor. Had Chad been outside while she was changing the snowAbby? Had he spied on her? And what was he going to do about it?

If he'd already told on her, her mother or Aunt Noreen would have been waiting for her. Abby was sure of that. No, he wouldn't tell, he'd just wait and do something to get even. He already had to get even for the smashed house, even though he deserved it. Abby went back to the kitchen to see if he was hiding there. McNab trotted along beside her, making snarly noises.

The kitchen and back hall were empty. If Chad had been there, he was gone now. The only wet shoes were her boots. McNab stood by the refrigerator, showing his teeth, so Abby gave him a cold biscuit before scurrying upstairs.

The sheets and pillowcases were like ice when Abby dived into bed. She pulled the covers up to her chin and tried not to shiver. Wind sprang up outside, howling around the tall stone house like a banshee trying to get in. It was the loneliest sound Abby had ever heard.

FOUR

*U*ncle Thomas's car woke Abby as he left for morning rounds at the hospital. She ran to the window to check her transformation of the snowAbby. Gone were the pigtails, the bows, the Abby face. It was now a snow-Chad with Chad's black hair, his inverted V eyebrows, a snowball clutched in the stick hand. But the best part was the huge coal teeth sticking out in a grin. There was no mistaking that look. It was Chad at his worst. Abby ran downstairs, eager for some reaction to the snowChad.

Nobody mentioned it, not even Chad. Abby could not tell if he hadn't noticed or just didn't want her to know he had. He shoveled snowdrifts off the front walk and went out with his sled. Nancy and Ginny brought theirs over with Ginny's little brother, Davy, a year younger than the twins. They bundled up and went out with their sled to play with him. Abby sat in the parlor watching them taking turns on the sleds, shrieking with laughter as they slid down the hill, until Aunt Noreen told her to join them.

"Sledding is the best of all winter fun," she said. "We all had names for our sleds when I was a girl. I called mine Comet."

"Mine was Blaze," Abby's mother said, and suddenly she looked like she did the last time the three of them went to the beach, before Daddy went overseas. "And I remember Tom's was Blizzard. We treated them like horses, racing them, stabling them in the back hall. My mother caught me trying to feed Blaze my bowl of cereal one morning. Tom called my sled Cheerio after that."

Abby put on her snow things and went out the front door to the cleared walk. Suddenly the earth turned to glass and her feet shot out from under her. She hung horizontally in the air for a moment before hitting the ground with a jarring *splat*. Abby lay still, wondering how many bones she had broken.

"Hey, you okay?" A face peered down at her. It was Ginny.

"I don't know." Abby didn't want to find out. She just wanted to lie there for a few years.

"Can you get up?"

"Probably not." Abby didn't know why Ginny was asking such a dumb question.

"Can you move your feet?"

She wished Ginny would go away. When Abby wanted to be friends with Ginny, she always ran off with Chad and Nancy. Why didn't she run off with them now? Abby planned to lie still until she froze so she couldn't feel any pain.

But Ginny wouldn't go away, so Abby tried to move her feet and discovered that they still worked.

"You just think everything is broken, but all those clothes padded you," Ginny said as she brushed packed snow off Abby's back.

"Thanks," Abby said.

"Walk around and you won't hurt after a few minutes."

Abby didn't believe her. She would never be able to walk again. But Ginny was right.

"Hey, Abby, want a turn?" Chad's sled was made of varnished wood with metal runners. He had stenciled its name, Flash, across it in red letters.

Abby didn't know how to sled, but he would call her names again if she didn't try. Besides, it looked like fun.

"What do I do?"

"Flop on your tum or sit up, hold on to the rope, and push off. Watch Nancy."

Nancy sat on her sled, similar to Chad's, and he gave her a push. She sailed off down the hill. Ginny and Davy went down together, lying on their stomachs on her sled.

"Do it on your tummy first," Polly said.

"It's easier," Patty said.

"How do you stop?"

"Brake with your feet," they said together.

Abby lay on the sled. "How do you guide it?"

"You don't, except by leaning," Chad said, handing her the useless rope. "It doesn't have reins like a horse. This is just to pull it by."

He gave her a mighty shove. The sled shot down the hill, skimming down the run packed by the other sleds. The snowbanks whizzed by. Icy air filled Abby's nose, her mouth. The sled gained momentum. She could see nothing now but a blur of white on each side. This was too fast. She couldn't control the sled. She didn't know where she was going. She was afraid she couldn't stop, she would turn over, veer into the path of something, a tree, a bush, a hidden rock, another sled. Abby dragged her feet. The sled slowed.

"Go faster!" Chad yelled. "Don't drag your feet."

But Abby didn't want to go faster. Half speed was fast enough. She stopped herself at the bottom. Her first sled ride wasn't fun. It was scary.

She pulled the sled back to the top, where Chad waited, grinning his sly know-it-all grin of superiority. "Why'd you go so slow?"

"It was fast enough for me."

"The whole point of sledding is to go fast. Scaredy-cat."

"Scaredy-cat," Nancy echoed. Then Ginny.

"Do you have to do everything Chad does?" Abby retorted, hiding her disappointment at Ginny's joining the teasing, acting just like the others. Even Davy was saying, "Thcaredy-cat." Only the twins said nothing. They were on their sled halfway down the hill.

Abby went back to the house. She'd had enough sledding.

Aunt Noreen was in the kitchen. "Tired already?"

"No, just cold. Where's Mom?"

"Oh, she's resting."

"Does she have a headache?"

"Oh, no. Want to help me make cookies for the kids?"

Abby didn't want to make anything for the kids except for the twins, but she liked Aunt Noreen and she liked cookies. She helped measure the flour and sugar.

Aunt Noreen gave her the pillowy oblong plastic package of white oleo with its little disk of yellow dye. Abby loved to break the disk and knead the yellow around, like spreading sunshine in the white until the whole package looked like soft real butter. Butter and sugar were rationed for the war, so they usually ate oleo. Sometimes Uncle Thomas's patients gave him ration coupons for sugar they didn't use and butter made from their cows, but Aunt Noreen saved that for meals. She said the patients did it because they appreciated Uncle Thomas coming to see them when they were sick in the middle of the night or for letting them pay him when they could. It was their way of saying thank you.

Aunt Noreen rolled the dough out on the white marble slab of the long kitchen table. She patted, then rolled the smooth floury pastry.

Abby cut out trees, bells, stars, and Santas with the cookie cutters and placed them on the sheets. The sledders came in as the cookies were cooling. Aunt Noreen made hot Ovaltine with milk and poured it into mugs. They sat at the long table in the breakfast nook and crunched the warm cookies. Davy bit off Santa's head. He would probably be just like Chad when he was older. The twins nibbled the edges of their cookies. Abby sat at the end of the table and felt left out as they talked about whose sled was the fastest and who almost went into the river and who just missed the elm tree. McNab pushed against Abby's leg. He showed his teeth and made a growly noise. Abby broke off cookie bits and dropped them for him. He pounced on them with a snarl.

The twins dragged Davy off to teach him their newest game, Rigamarroolulu.

"These are great cookies," Ginny said.

"Abby made them," Aunt Noreen said.

"I hereby dub Abby the greatest cookie maker in the world!" Chad said, touching Abby on the head and shoulders with a tree cookie while Nancy and Ginny giggled.

Abby wasn't fooled. He was only doing it to show off.

"I think you should make cookies every day," he added.

"We have to save the sugar for our Christmas baking," Aunt Noreen said.

Abby waited for one of them to mention the snow-Chad, but they began to talk about Christmas. "Maybe you'll see the ghost this year," Nancy said.

"Aw, you say that every year," Chad said. "There's no such thing."

"There is," Nancy said emphatically, crumbs dropping off the corner of her mouth as she nodded.

"In three years we've never seen any ghosts," Chad said.

"Maybe you have to look for it," Ginny said.

"What ghost?" Abby asked.

Nancy leaned across the table and spoke in a spooky voice. "The ghost of a girl about our age. She lived in this house during the Civil War. She drowned and comes back at Christmastime. Nobody knows why."

Abby stared at Nancy. It sounded like a story from a book, but Nancy looked like she believed it. Her cheeks were pink from sledding. Her light brown hair was still mashed down from her hat. Her brown eyes opened wide as she told the story. "She wears a red velvet dress."

"I don't believe it," Abby said.

"It's true," Ginny said. Her hair was almost the same color as Nancy's but longer and she had blue eyes that sparkled at the story. She didn't have to sleep in a haunted house. "When she was little, my grandmother knew the family that lived here. They had a daughter about her age. She said she saw the ghost. It had blonde hair and wore a red dress that was wet."

"I don't believe it either," Chad said. "You're making it up."

"It's true," Ginny said. "Do you believe in ghosts?" she asked Abby.

"I don't know," Abby said. "I've never seen one."

"Maybe now you will," Nancy said.

"I hope not." Abby didn't want to see a ghost. Maybe you couldn't if you didn't believe in them. Chad said he'd never seen one and didn't believe anybody else had. To be on the safe side, she decided not to believe in ghosts either. For once, she agreed with Chad.

FIVE

*U*ncle Thomas came home early and, without taking off his hat, stood in the hall, calling, "Christmas tree time! Everybody get ready and let's go."

Abby and Chad and the twins and Aunt Noreen bundled into their warmest clothes and piled into the Buick. Uncle Thomas threw ropes, an old quilt, a sled, and a saw into the trunk. Abby wished her mother would come, but she said she had things to do and smiled mysteriously. Abby guessed it had something to do with Christmas presents.

They had mailed a Christmas box to Dad in September, before he was reported missing. Abby had made him a little booklet of her life, with drawings from school and other activities, snapshots of herself and her mother and their house glued on, as well as pressed flowers and leaves from their yard in Florida, even some sand and tiny seashells from the beach. Abby had been afraid the booklet would make him miss them too much, but her mother said it would bring them closer to him. They had saved their ration coupons to make him a small fruitcake and a pan of fudge and tucked in salted pecans. Now they didn't know if he would ever receive his Christmas box. Abby hoped he would. Nobody had sent it back to them. She hoped the Nazis didn't get it.

Abby had to sit next to Chad in the backseat because Patty got carsick sitting in the middle and Polly had to sit next to her and Chad insisted on a window. Abby squirmed to find a comfortable spot. Chad's elbows seemed to dig into her ribs no matter how she sat. "Seat hog," she muttered under her breath. McNab glowered up at her from the floor between her legs and Chad's. Why did they have to bring that dog along to cut a tree? He was in the way, but Chad had insisted. "He always goes with us," he said.

"But there's not enough room," Abby said.

"That's not his fault," Chad said, meaning that she was taking McNab's space.

Uncle Thomas sang Christmas carols in his deep baritone and they all sang along with him on the way to the woods that belonged to one of his patients. Chad stepped on Abby's foot as they piled out of the car but said it was an accident.

The woods were quiet and still, the snow-laden branches of the evergreen trees bent low. The sun glowed behind milky clouds that promised snow and gave the woods a frosty fairy-tale look as they tramped through the snow, looking for the perfect tree. McNab ran around, barking at snow-covered bushes.

"He thinks they're bears," Polly said.

"And wolves," Patty said.

Abby wouldn't have been surprised to see a snow queen or elves or Santa Claus. But when something jumped out at her, it was only Chad followed by a shower of snow as he shook the branches of a pine tree.

The woods seemed to hum with a droning noise.

"A plane!" squealed Polly.

"Germans!" screamed Patty.

"Take cover!" Chad yelled.

Abby dived under a tree with the twins and McNab and peered through its needled branches. The plane was silver against the clouds, headed east.

"A Messerschmitt!" Chad shouted. "It's a Messer-schmitt!"

"No, Chad, it's a Mustang," Uncle Thomas said, pointing. "See the star on the wing?"

Chad squinted at the plane. "Oh, yeah, it's one of ours. A P-62. I knew that."

Abby and the twins disentangled themselves from the branches. McNab got off her foot. She hoped the plane was flying to Europe to protect her dad from the Germans.

"I knew it was a P-62," Chad told her, tipping another branch to spray her with snow.

"Then why did you say it was a Messerschmitt?" Abby said.

"I was testing you," Chad said with his left eyebrow raised. Abby wanted to smack him.

"Who can find the tallest tree?" Uncle Thomas asked.

"Me. I can," said Polly.

"This one," Patty said, pointing at a tree in front of her.

"No, this one," Polly said, pointing at another.

"We want a tall one," Aunt Noreen said.

"And a fat one," Uncle Thomas added.

The tree they finally chose was a six-foot spruce. Uncle Thomas made a cut about two feet up the trunk, leaving some branches so it would grow another tree in a hurry, he said. Everybody took a turn with the saw until the tree fell with a crack. They cut more branches from other trees and holly to decorate the house and loaded it all on the sled.

"This is a Christmas car," Polly said as Uncle

Thomas strapped the tree onto the roof. Abby and Chad put the greenery in the trunk. She wished she could put Chad in there, too. And McNab.

"A Merry Christmas car," Patty added.

"Dashing through the snow," Uncle Thomas sang, leading the singing on the way home, and Abby felt happier than she had since the telegram came about her dad, even with Chad's elbow and feet getting in her way. She elbowed him back.

Uncle Thomas parked in the garage. Abby and Chad and the twins carried the tree into the house and stood it in the middle of the parlor as Aunt Noreen brought out boxes of decorations. Abby's mother put a record on the Victrola and Christmas music filled the house.

"Abby, you get to put on the star this year," Uncle Thomas said. Abby climbed the stepladder he held for her and fastened the big silver star onto the top of the tree.

"My dad and I always put a starfish on top of our tree," she said.

"Aw, that's dumb," Chad said. "Whoever heard of a starfish on a Christmas tree?"

Abby didn't say anything. It had been her dad's idea. In Florida everybody thought it was clever.

"I think that's original," Aunt Noreen said. Uncle

Thomas put lights on the branches and then divided the tree into zones. The twins hung balls on the lower branches while Abby and Chad each were assigned a side of the upper tree.

Chad and the twins hung the balls any old way. "You're supposed to hang the big ones close to the trunk, medium ones in the middle, and the tiny ones on the tip," Abby said. She and her dad had always decorated their tree together. He always said it was a work of art.

The twins immediately rearranged theirs, but Chad refused. "I put 'em where I think they should go."

"They don't go there." Abby moved a large purple ball from the tip of a limb where it could slide off.

Chad put the ball back. The branch drooped under its weight. "But it might fall off there or get knocked off," Abby said.

"No, it won't." Chad bent the hook around the branch.

Abby showed the twins how to put the used icicles on the branches, straightening them first by sliding them gently between two fingernails, "like you're ironing them," then hanging them one strand at a time from the inside of the limb to the end.

Chad threw wads of icicles at the tree. "Bombs away!" he shouted as he let fly. McNab leaped to catch it. A wad hit the star.

Abby ignored him.

The next wad hit her in the ear.

"Bull's-eye!" Chad said with a grin.

She caught it and smoothed the icicles out, draping them on a branch. Chad continued to throw icicles at the tree with McNab jumping around until there were no more left. The clunky wads didn't shimmer. They ruined the tree. She would straighten them later.

McNab pulled an icicle off a low branch and ran around with it hanging out of his mouth.

"He thinks he's a Christmas dog," Chad said. The twins laughed. Even Abby had to admit he was funny.

"Let's make the village," Polly said.

"Abby can help us," Patty said.

They stood on chairs and spread a sheet of cotton along the length of the mantel. Abby helped them unwrap the little cardboard houses and tiny china figurines for the snowy village scene. "I have an idea," she said and ran upstairs for a pocket mirror from an old handbag. She nestled it into the cotton to make a little frozen pond. Polly and Patty put two skaters, a girl and a boy, on it. Abby added a dog to the mirror. She bet McNab would never put his paw on the ice, but this dog, a brown spaniel, was nicer than McNab. It didn't growl or frown or steal decorations off the tree.

Chad put the houses and church in a row in the middle of the mantel. The twins set more villagers walking along the street, caroling, carrying packages and little trees. Abby laid leftover tree branches on each end for woods. "I wish we had some snow for the forest," she said.

"We know how to make snow," Polly said.

"We did it at school," Patty added.

They ran to the kitchen and came back with handfuls of dry Lux soap flakes, which they sprinkled on the branches and village rooftops.

"It looks just like real snow," Polly said.

"Falling on the Christmas tree forest," Patty said.

"Just like real clean snow," Chad said, making the twins laugh. "The cleanest snow in town."

"Supper," Aunt Noreen called.

All the grown-ups said it was the most beautiful tree they'd ever seen, but Abby wanted it to be perfect. She wanted to straighten the snarls of icicles. She waited for Chad to go upstairs after supper to work on his matchstick house. But he played checkers with the twins, first with Polly, then with Patty until bedtime.

Abby lingered on the stairs, but he stayed behind, too. "Want to go on a ghost watch?" he whispered.

"A what?"

"Shhh. Don't scare them." He nodded at the twins. "A ghost watch. To catch the Christmas ghost."

"You mean like catching Santa Claus?"

"Sort of. Except ghosts probably want to get caught. Why else would they appear?"

"I don't know. I've never met a ghost." And she wasn't eager to meet one now.

"I'll bet you'll see one here." Chad grinned and his eyebrows went up. "This is a spooky old house. Remember what Nancy said. Maybe we'll catch the Christmas ghost."

Abby gave him a suspicious look. "I thought you didn't believe in ghosts."

"Nancy and Ginny convinced me. Well, do you?"

"No, I don't."

"Scaredy-cat."

"I am not."

"Are, too. You're scared of the dark."

Abby thought about her adventure alone in the dark last night. She wasn't afraid. She was planning to come back down later tonight and redo the tree. But she was tired of him calling her names. "Oh, all right. If it will shut you up. What do we do?"

"Meet me at the bottom of the stairs."

"When?"

He raised his eyebrows. "At midnight. When else?"

"Midnight is awfully late. Why then?"

"That's when ghosts walk. Don't you know any-thing?"

"I know lots of things but not about ghosts. I don't believe in them."

He grinned a fiendish grin, then stuck his teeth out and crossed his eyes. "Maybe you will after tonight."

Abby put on pajamas, bed socks, and robe after her bath. She was ready for the ghost watch. She settled down in bed and opened her book.

At eleven Abby finished reading *Ivanhoe*. She decided to go downstairs early and rearrange icicles while she waited for Chad.

McNab crawled out from under her bed as she opened the door. She hadn't even known he was under there. He was getting sneakier. She would have to watch him more carefully. What if she'd gotten up to go to the bathroom and he had bitten her foot? "Get out of there, you awful dog."

McNab grumbled as he followed her into the hall. The house was the darkest place she'd ever seen, with all the windows blacked out. "Chad?" she whispered.

No answer. The house was silent except for the ticking of the grandfather clock. Abby felt her way down the stairs. She would turn on the lamp in the hall. If Uncle Thomas was out late on a house call, he should have a light left on for him. If he wasn't, Abby reasoned, the house needed a light because it was spooky.

As Abby reached the last step, something made a noise on the stairs above her. A shuffling noise.

"Chad, is that you?"

No answer.

Don't be afraid, she told herself. Remember what Dad said. Analyze the situation. A ghost can't hurt you. You don't have to be afraid of a ghost.

Something furry touched her ankle. McNab. Abby snatched her foot back and turned to go around him and then she saw the white shape at the top of the stairs. It was time to scream.

SIX

*A*bby tried to scream but nothing came out. She closed her eyes. She had imagined the thing. But when she opened them, the white shape was still there, luminous as it glided slowly across the landing above her.

"I am the Christmas ghost," it said.

Abby opened her mouth, but her throat didn't work anymore, and the noises that came out sounded like she was choking.

"I have come ba-a-a-ack," the ghost whispered, "to right a terrible wro-o-o-ng."

Abby leaned against the banister as she struggled to catch her breath. The ghostly shape moved slowly, drifting down the stairs toward her.

The hall clock's ticktocks sounded like gunshots in

the silence as Abby clung to the banister and backed away.

The ghost floated above her, relentlessly following. And then it moaned.

"Oooooooooh."

Abby thought she would faint.

"Oooooooooh," the mournful voice sounded again.

The ghost came closer. Abby couldn't move. She was paralyzed. It was going to get her.

Something thumped her leg. She flinched as if she had been touched by a ghost. A furry ghost. But it was only McNab, wagging his tail. He wasn't afraid of the ghost.

Analyze the situation, Abby told herself. A dog wouldn't wag its tail at a ghost. McNab especially wouldn't. He didn't wag his tail at anybody except . . .

Abby pretended to be in a trance. "Oh, wait, Christmas ghost, I am coming. I want to come with you." She moved up a step. The ghost hovered for a second, as if uncertain of its direction. Abby took another step. The ghost moaned again, but Abby didn't back down.

"Ooooooh noooooh! Ooooooooh noooooooooh!" the ghost moaned, waving an arm and backing up the stairs.

As Abby advanced up the stairs, the ghost retreated, but it tried to do so in a manner that was dignified to a ghost. Abby was under no such constraints. She took the stairs two at a time, chanting, "I'm coming, oh Christmas ghost, wait for me, I'm coming."

At the top of the stairs the ghost tried to run, but Abby caught the corner of Aunt Noreen's white bedsheet and flipped it off the ghost. Chad stood revealed, holding a flashlight under his chin.

"Ha! Got you," she said.

"I scared you good," Chad said, triumphant.

"You didn't scare me one little bit," Abby said. "I knew it was you, you skunk!"

"You did not."

"I did."

"How?"

"McNab. He gave you away wagging his tail. If you'd been a real ghost he would have been scared."

"No, he wouldn't. McNab's not afraid of anything. He would have attacked the ghost."

The exhilaration of catching Chad gradually ebbed and Abby felt a slow anger take its place. "It was a mean trick," she told him.

"Help me fold up the sheet," Chad said.

"I will not. Fold it up yourself. What if one of the twins had seen you?"

"The twins are always together so they're never scared," Chad said as he wrestled with the sheet. "They don't even go to the bathroom alone. Besides, I would have heard them first. But if they had seen me, I would have taken the sheet off right away. You should've waited until midnight like I told you. You would have really been scared then."

"I would not. I would have known it was you then, too."

He gave up on the sheet, wadded it, and threw it into the hall linen closet on his way back to his room, leaving Abby in the dark with McNab. She went back to her room and had reached her door as the hall clock struck the half hour, eleven-thirty. She remembered she hadn't turned on the light for Uncle Thomas and started back downstairs. McNab followed.

"Go back, McNab," Abby told him.

McNab peered at her through his hair and showed his bottom teeth in a snarl, but he didn't growl this time.

Abby went down the stairs and crossed the hall. The table with the lamp was halfway to the front door. She'd left the door to her room ajar, but the light didn't penetrate the darkness downstairs. She bumped the edge of the table and reached to turn on the lamp. Just as she touched the switch, shadows receded from the light, and she thought she saw a flash of something red, a blur of blonde hair from the corner of her eye. It looked like a girl.

She blinked and turned to look again, but the girl

was gone. She must have been hiding in the hall shadows. Wet footprints led from the front door straight to the parlor. The girl must have come in while she was upstairs with Chad and run past her just as she switched on the lamp.

She would find out who it was this time. Abby followed the footprints down the hall to the parlor. She turned on the parlor lamp but the room was empty. The footprints trailed damply across the rug to the sofa where they turned, as if somebody had sat down. There the footprints stopped.

Abby searched the room. It had to be one of the twins or maybe both. Maybe they were hiding in the parlor. Abby looked behind the furniture, behind the heavy velvet curtains, in the window seat, behind the bookcase. No twins. She looked under the tree, where a small twin could crouch. The branches shimmered with their icicles and balls, but no one was hidden there. Abby decided that one of the twins had been trying to go back upstairs unseen, through the parlor to the dining room and up the back stairs.

"Polly? Patty?" Abby called softly as she walked through the rooms. No reply. The kitchen was empty. She went back to the parlor, then to the hall. McNab stood with his hackles up, his eyes on the front door, as though he expected someone or something to come through it.

Abby checked the latch. It was securely locked. Nobody could come through that door without a key.

"Go to bed, McNab," she told him.

He made a low growly sound. Later, just as she was drifting off to sleep, she heard him sniffling about outside her door.

SEVEN

*A*bby watched the miniature train circle a Christmas tree in the window of Bartley's Department Store while her mother and Aunt Noreen shopped inside. A family of mannequins modeled pajamas and robes and slippers. Abby turned away, thinking of Christmases when her daddy was home with them.

The town of Stratton Falls was as disappointing as the window of its leading store. At home, even in wartime, the stores were festive with giant paper snowflakes hanging from ceilings and greenery decorated with snowflakes and silver balls looped across balconies. Goldbaum's, her favorite, had real live models in a Christmas scene in its window, and carols played on a loudspeaker. Christmas was more fun in Jacksonville even if there was no snow. They had the beach and more stores than Stratton Falls with its business district of three blocks and one cross street. Bartley's, the biggest store in town, was draped with patriotic red, white, and blue bunting and flags. It looked more like the Fourth of July than Christmas.

Chad and the twins were in Denton's Five and Dime, where Abby planned to go next. Bartley's didn't have toys, only clothes and shoes and sewing things— bolts of cloth, thread, needles, patterns, and pins. Abby leaned against the window. Why were they taking so long?

Finally her mother emerged. "We haven't finished yet," she said. "But you can go on and do your shopping." She gave Abby two dollars. "This should be enough."

"But I have to buy a lot of presents," Abby protested, ticking them off on her fingers, "for Polly and Patty and Aunt Noreen and Uncle Thomas and you."

"Don't forget Chad."

"Chad? I'm not going to buy him anything. He's too mean. He should only get a bag of switches or lumps of coal," Abby said, thinking about last night's ghost trick.

Her mother sighed. "Now, Abby. It's Christmas. Be more charitable. He's just a typical boy. Remember, we're staying at his house. And he is your cousin."

"He is not. He's not my cousin."

"He is by marriage. Step-cousin. He's Polly's and Patty's brother and they love him. Think how upset they will be if he doesn't get a present from you."

"He's nice to the twins. That's why they love him. If he was as mean to them as he is to me, they wouldn't love him. They wouldn't even like him. They would hate him like I do." Abby got mad all over again thinking of Chad's tricks.

"It's Christmas, Abby. Try to remember that," her mother reminded her with a smile. But she gave Abby another dollar.

"I'll buy him a present because of Polly and Patty and Aunt Noreen and Uncle Thomas. But that's the only reason. Just it being Christmas isn't enough."

Abby put the folded bills into her pocket as she hurried to Denton's, where the windows held an assortment of the things for sale inside, mostly grown-up things that she wasn't interested in, like brooms, mops, clothes, toiletries, and one wooden doll in a wooden bed. Abby was prepared for the wooden skates and other wooden toys. After three years of the war, all metal was used for tanks and jeeps and trucks and ships and submarines. Clothes were rationed because cotton and wool were used to make uniforms for the soldiers and sailors and nurses and marines. And for bandages. But Abby didn't want to think about those. Her daddy wasn't wounded. He couldn't be. She refused to believe anything bad had happened to him. If she didn't think it, it wouldn't be true.

Denton's smelled like candy and popcorn. Abby spent a long time looking. She wanted to get something special for her mother to cheer her up. This was the first Christmas she hadn't had a present from Abby's dad. He wouldn't be able to send her anything, so it was up to Abby to buy one for him. She looked at two- and three-piece gift sets with perfume, cologne, and bath powder for $3.00, $4.50, and $5.00. Even if she bought the cheapest one, she wouldn't have enough left over. Strings of pearls were $1.00 and $2.00. A lacy fascinator to put over hair was $1.97, and scarves were 41 cents to $1.95. Abby was torn between a moss green scarf with tiny pink roses and a string of pearls.

If she was careful, she might be able to get the one-strand pearls and the scarf. Abby bought a set of celluloid bath toys—two red fish, a purple turtle, and a blue frog—all for only ten cents, and two books not much bigger than her hand, *Jemima Puddle-Duck* and *The Tailor of Gloucester* by Beatrix Potter, which she knew the twins didn't have, for five cents each. She could divide the bath toys and wrap them separately to make lots of little presents for the twins to open. They would like that.

Uncle Thomas was a problem. Abby didn't know what to get for him. He seemed to have everything he wanted or needed. She considered candy but didn't know what kind he liked. Ties were $1.00; three-piece men's toiletry sets were $3.00. Too expensive. Finally, Abby found a ten-cent carved wooden picture frame that he could put three pictures in, one of each of his children, for his office desk.

For Aunt Noreen she bought a pale green hankie with a narrow white lace border made in Ireland, only twenty-nine cents. Abby looked for a ball for McNab, but rubber was just as scarce as everything else because all those jeeps and trucks had to have tires.

Abby counted her money. She had spent fifty-nine cents and had $2.41 left. She bought the $1.00 pearls in the narrow satin-lined box. She would put her dad's name on them. Then she bought the scarf for $1.29 from her. She was left with twelve cents to spend on Chad. It was more than he deserved.

There weren't many toys that cost a dime or less, and the only ones suitable for Chad were model planes. But Abby didn't know which models he already had. They all looked the same to her. She ignored the little soldiers and other war toys. She hated war too much to buy war toys. She picked up a wooden flute and a wooden top. Chad would hate those. It would be fun to give him a present he wouldn't like.

Abby weighed the top in her hand, then changed

her mind. The grown-ups might suspect. She looked at the books. They were acceptable presents to grown-ups, but Chad probably wouldn't like getting one. She had never seen him reading anything but the comic strips in the newspaper. Abby looked at each book, but they were all for younger children. She asked a clerk if they had any books for older readers.

"No, these are all we have. But you might try the secondhand bookstore around the corner."

Abby thanked her and hurried out to the street. A light snow was falling, like little rice grains. They made tiny pinging sounds when they hit rooftops and pavement. She passed the Rialto Theater next door, where *Going My Way*, with Bing Crosby and Rise Stevens, was playing. Abby had seen it with her mother months ago in Jacksonville, but it was just now showing here. Jacksonville seemed like a million miles away from Stratton Falls.

Around the corner she found a tiny store with a carved sign over the door that read DICKENS AND FRIENDS. A card in a window display read "Books bought and sold, none too cheap and none too dear, but all the books here are gold."

The store was crammed with books on shelves from floor to ceiling and, between the aisles, in stacks almost as tall as she was. Abby didn't know where to start when a stooped man with white hair appeared from behind a counter piled with books and said, "Tell me what you are looking for and I'll find it for you."

"I'm looking for a book about a bad boy," Abby confided.

"Oh ho. Like that, is it? Hmmm. Well, there are plenty of those. How old?" asked the man, rummaging around in the piles behind the stacks of books.

"Almost thirteen. I only have twelve cents," Abby said with embarrassment. She hadn't meant to end up with so little for Chad, even if she didn't like him.

"Well, there's *Peck's Bad Boy.* And here's *Penrod and Sam,* by Booth Tarkington. It was very popular in—oh, about 1916. They're both in good shape, like new, no writing in them, and each costs just one dime." He flipped through the pages of each book so Abby could see for herself. They looked like new.

Abby considered. She preferred *Peck's Bad Boy,* but it sounded too much like what she thought of Chad. "I'll take the Penrod one," she said, happy that her problem was solved. The book was nice and thick, so it wouldn't look like it cost only a dime, and it had pictures. The grown-ups would think it was a good present, and Chad would hate it!

Abby paid her dime and thanked the man as she hid the book at the bottom of her bag of presents. She had two cents left and bought two peppermint sticks for the twins.

"Wait till you see what I got you," Chad said on the way home. Something awful no doubt. Aunt Noreen had bought red and white and green tissue paper and colored cord and Christmas seals. She collected scissors, glue, crayons, and paper for them to make cards. Abby made the twins wait outside the kitchen while she wrapped their presents first. They squealed over the piles.

"All for us!" Patty exclaimed.

"We love little presents," Polly said.

Abby helped them wrap theirs, glass figurines for their mother, a big box of candy for Chad, and a china monkey for their father. She wrapped Chad's book in case he came snooping around. Just as she was tying the green cord in a bow, he bounded in to wrap his, McNab at his heels. The snarly dog lay down beside Abby's chair.

When Chad and the twins made her leave while they wrapped her presents, McNab trotted after her. She put the presents under the tree, then rearranged balls and untangled clumps of icicles until everyone shouted for her to come back.

Chad and the twins admired the scarf and string of pearls, even the box they came in.

"You should put pictures in the frame for Daddy," Polly said.

"So he'll know who is supposed to be in it," Patty said.

They ran to their room to pick one of each of them and one of Chad for Abby to slip into the frame. She had to admit that the frame looked nicer with the pictures.

"You should have got one with four places for pictures," Polly said.

"So you could be in it, too," Patty said.

"I didn't see any," Abby said. She wasn't Uncle Thomas's daughter. She had a father she had sent pictures to, but she didn't know if he would ever see them. Abby tried not to think about that as she helped the twins draw and color Christmas trees and wreaths on cards to put on each present.

Chad drew a round Santa and cross-eyed reindeer that made the twins scream with laughter. "Draw funny Santas and reindeers on our cards," they begged. He drew a beanpole Santa for Polly and one stuffed with pillows for Patty.

Abby drew a palm tree with Santa fanning himself. Then she drew reindeer with sunglasses and Santa going down the chimney of a boat.

"Doesn't it ever snow where you lived?" Patty asked.

"In Florida," Polly added.

"No. Not ever," Abby told them.

"Is it warm on Christmas?" Patty asked.

"Do you go swimming in the winter?" Polly asked.

"It's warm, but not hot. Some people go swimming in the winter, but I never did. It's not that warm." Abby drew a sleigh with McNab, wearing antlers, pulling it.

Chad drew McNab in a Santa suit. They were having such fun and Chad was being so nice that Abby felt guilty about buying him a present he wouldn't like and almost guilty for the snowChad. But she felt the guiltiest about breaking the house he was building for the twins. When they left for him to wrap their presents, she asked him if he had finished it.

"No," he said, without looking at her. "I don't have enough matchsticks. I'll finish it when I get some more. I bought them little dolls. Here, put your finger on the bow."

Abby stuck her finger in the bow and wished she had some matchsticks to give him. The twins would be so excited to have a dollhouse with dolls to live in it. She had spoiled their Christmas with her fit of temper at Chad. He had caused it, but she shouldn't have thrown her book at him. And now he wasn't even being mean about it. "Did you get furniture, too?"

"No," he said, slipping the card under the ribbon.

"Denton's didn't have any. Maybe I can get them some for their birthday in July."

Abby was about to say that he could make some when she thought of a way to make up for breaking the house. She would make some furniture out of cardboard and pillboxes and bottle tops and whatever else she could find. She knew how to make rocking chairs and regular chairs and beds. She was sure Aunt Noreen would give her scraps for bedclothes and curtains and upholstery and spools for lamps with fluted paper shades made from the cups in a candy box. It would be fun. She would start tonight. She would surprise the twins and Chad, too.

As they set the table for supper, Chad was back to his old tricks. "Shouldn't we set an extra place at the table?"

"What for?" Abby counted the places. "There are seven."

"You know. For the ghost."

"What ghost?" Abby glanced across the table at him. His left eyebrow went up into his floppy hair and he grinned. "The one Nancy told us about that comes at Christmas."

"The only ghost in this house is you in a sheet."

"I wouldn't be too sure about that."

What was he cooking up now? Abby stopped placing the silverware. She decided to play along and see.

"Well, if you think there's really a ghost in this house, I guess we'll have to go on another ghost watch. Together this time, so you can't sneak around and play any tricks."

"If you're not too scared."

Abby plunked down a fork at Uncle Thomas's place. It clanged against the plate. She straightened it. "I'm not scared of any ghost."

"Oh yeah? We'll see about that."

EIGHT

*W*hen the downstairs clock chimed the half hour after ten, Abby crossed the hall to Chad's room to make sure he didn't pull his ghost trick again. He was on the floor in his pajamas and robe, gluing matchsticks on the dollhouse. McNab snoozed on the bed.

"I thought you didn't have any more matchsticks."

"Dad brought me some from his patients. I don't have nearly enough, but if he brings me a few every day, I should finish the house by New Year's."

Abby looked at his room. This was the first time she had been in it. He had a sign on the door. KEEP OUT— THIS MEANS YOU with a skull and crossbones underneath, and she had never wanted to come in where she wasn't wanted. His room was bigger than hers. A rag rug covered most of the floor. Three model airplanes hung on strings from his ceiling. She only recognized the B-52 bomber. "What are the other two?"

"American Mustang and a British Spitfire."

A desk under a window was piled with schoolbooks and notebooks and messy papers. More books were crammed into a bookcase with games. A collection of miniature cannons and soldiers paraded across his dresser and windowsill. A picture of a jungle tiger hung over his bed. His curtains were blue checked and his bed was covered with a crazy quilt.

"What are you doing here so early?" Chad asked. "The ghost won't walk until midnight. It's not even eleven yet."

"I know. I came to make sure you don't play ghost again."

"I won't have to. I bet we see a real ghost." He put the last matchstick in place, then shoved the house under his bed. "We have time for Parcheesi," he said.

They played until after eleven. McNab snored on the bed. Abby stifled a yawn as she helped pick up the game pieces. She closed the lid on the box. "Let's go down now," she said. "In case the ghost is early."

McNab jumped up, but they made him stay in the

room. "He'll bark at the ghost and wake everybody up," Chad said.

The hall was dark. Chad didn't want to turn on the overhead hall light. "It spoils the effect," he said, "and might scare the ghost away."

Abby insisted they leave a lamp on upstairs. "We won't be able to find our way around in the dark."

As they went down the stairs her eyes adjusted to the lessening light. The back of her neck tingled as she waited for Chad to jump at her and say "Gotcha" or try to scare her some other way. But he was quiet.

"Where should we look?" she asked.

"I don't know. How about the parlor?"

Abby prepared herself for Nancy or Ginny or both wrapped in bedsheets moaning whoo whoo whoo. Or the twins.

The tree ornaments gleamed in the muted light from the upstairs lamp. Abby checked the window seat with the blackout curtains. No ghost there.

The fireplace chairs were empty, too. She moved to the side of the tree and looked beyond it to the sofa. Chad was right by her. Suddenly he clutched her arm and made a strangled noise and at the same time Abby saw it, too.

Chad's fingers tightened on Abby's arm. Her heart hammered in her chest. Chad made choking sounds.

"She's real!" he gasped. Then he turned and ran, his footsteps thudding all the way up the stairs to his room.

The figure on the sofa didn't move.

Abby stood rooted to the rug. The girl was still, her eyes cast down, hands folded in her lap.

Remember there are two ways of looking at this, Abby told herself. Either it's somebody pretending to be a ghost. Or—it's a ghost. A real ghost.

The girl wasn't Polly or Patty or Nancy or Ginny. She was no one Abby had ever seen before. She had long blonde hair. And she was wearing a red velvet dress.

The room swam, the tree spun, and Abby thought she would faint. She took several deep breaths, closed her eyes tightly, then opened them again. The girl was still there. She didn't seem threatening. And nothing had happened to Abby. She had to be a real girl, somebody Chad had sneaked into the house to pretend to be a ghost. Please be real, Abby hoped to herself.

Abby found her voice. "Who . . . who are you?"

The girl ignored her.

"Who are you?" Abby asked again in a louder tone.

The girl didn't answer. She continued to ignore Abby. She was a good actress. Ginny or Nancy would be giggling by now if they were involved. But this girl didn't giggle. She didn't seem to know that Abby was there. Her dress was old-fashioned, cut in princess style that buttoned all the way down the front with a high neck and long sleeves. The shoulders, sleeves, neck, and hem were trimmed with black braid that gave it a military look. The girl wore white stockings above black boots with little black buttons. They looked wet, and then Abby saw the wet footprints on the rug in front of the girl and remembered the prints from the night before. For a moment she was so scared she couldn't even breathe. The ghost sat primly with her ankles together, her hands folded, her eyes down. The red dress seemed to cling to her, as if it, too, were wet. The girl raised her head.

But before her eyes reached Abby's, the ghost began to fade, first her boots, then her skirt, her hands, her shoulders, and last her face until two spots of blue hung in the air and then they, too, disappeared.

Abby saw it but she didn't believe it. The girl was there and then she wasn't. How was that possible?

It wasn't. Unless she really was a ghost.

The lamp seemed a million miles away as Abby, desperate for light, ran to the table on the other side of the room and fumbled for the switch between the two globes of ruby-colored glass. With a click the room became the friendly parlor again, the tree she'd helped decorate centered on the Oriental rug, the snowy village on the mantel, the plump pillows on the window seat where she liked to read, the blackout curtains pulled to-gether. The girl was gone, but on the floor, Abby saw the trail of wet footprints. She followed them to the front door where they began.

And then Abby knew the girl was a ghost.

*C*had avoided Abby at breakfast, keeping his head down as he swirled blackberry jam into his oatmeal, making patterns until it all turned lavender. Abby didn't mention the ghost in front of the twins as they washed the dishes and put them away. As soon as they finished, Chad put on his warm clothes and ran outside. Abby put hers on, too, and carefully picked her way across the snow in front of the house. Chad was throwing snowballs at the snowChad. He had already knocked off the nose and teeth.

"Chad, you shouldn't have run off last night. That was a real ghost in the parlor."

He threw another snowball. It knocked off an eye.

"Bull's-eye!" he shouted.

Abby stamped her boot. "Chad, did you hear me?"

He hefted a snowball as he faced her. His face was red under his stocking cap. "I heard you. But I don't believe you. I didn't see any ghost last night. You made it up."

"I did not! You saw her."

"Didn't."

For a moment Abby doubted what she had seen. Maybe it had been a trick? Chad could have pretended to be scared of the ghost so she would think it was real and then today denied it. Abby remembered the girl in the dark red velvet dress. She had seen her. It wasn't a trick.

"We both saw her," Abby insisted.

"I didn't see anything."

"Then why did you run away?"

"I went to bed. I was sleepy." He scooped a handful of snow. But Abby didn't back down. She knew what she had seen. Why wouldn't he admit he had seen it, too?

"You saw her, Chad. I know you did. You saw her."

"Saw what?" It was Nancy followed by Ginny, who echoed her. "Saw what?"

"The Christmas ghost. The girl you told us about, the one in the red dress. I saw her last night!" Abby told them. "Chad did, too. But now he won't admit it."

"I did not!" Chad yelled, his face even redder.

"You did. You nearly squeezed my arm off. He grabbed hold of me he was so scared, and then he ran off upstairs."

"Didnotdidnotdidnot!" Chad chanted. He threw a snowball as hard as he could, catching her full in the face. Abby sputtered and almost fell backward. She wiped the snow out of her eyes, spitting out a mouthful of snow. She picked up a handful to make a ball.

"C'mon, everybody, let's get her!" Chad yelled, pelting Abby fast with quick hard balls. Abby lobbed her ball at Chad, catching him on the shoulder. Her back flinched as she expected Nancy and Ginny to attack from behind.

Two snowballs whizzed by her and hit Chad in the face and stomach. He stopped in surprise as Nancy and Ginny let fly and hit him again. Abby made another snowball and caught him squarely in his open mouth, and before he could throw again, Nancy and Ginny hit him in both knees.

As he spat snow, he yelled, "No fair, three against one, no fair!"

The snowballs didn't stop until he ran away—still yelling "No fair!"—to safety behind the garage.

"Come on, let's go to my house," Nancy said.

Nancy's house was next door, but they had to tramp across a wide field of snow crisscrossed with tracks. Her mother was baking in the kitchen, but she let them pop corn and make hot Ovaltine to take to Nancy's room.

"Tell us about the ghost," Nancy said as they sat on blue scatter rugs.

First, Abby told them about Chad's trick and the wet footprints.

"Ooooh," Ginny said, anticipating what was coming.

"Double ooooh," Nancy said, scooping up popcorn.

"Behind the Christmas tree, sitting on the sofa with her hands folded, sat the Christmas ghost," Abby said in a spooky voice.

"What did she do?" Ginny interrupted.

"She didn't do anything," Abby said. They looked disappointed. She told them what Chad did, adding a few embellishments. "He sounded like a reindeer herd galloping up the stairs. Then I asked the girl who she was."

"You spoke to her? Out loud?" Nancy seemed impressed.

"Twice. 'Who are you?' I asked her. She didn't answer. She didn't even seem to know I was there. And then she started to fade."

"Ooooh," Ginny let her breath out.

"You mean she just disappeared?" Nancy asked.

Abby nodded. "She evaporated. Her eyes went last."

"I would've been so scared," Nancy said.

"Did she make any noise?" Ginny asked.

"No, not a sound. I don't know how long I stood there. Until she was all faded away. I turned on the light. The sofa looked a little damp, and the trail of wet footprints only led from the front door to the sofa but not back again."

"Golly," Ginny said. "That was really spooky."

"Do you think she's still in the house?" Nancy asked.

Abby thought for a minute. "I don't know."

"I wish I could see a real ghost," Ginny said.

"No, you don't," Nancy told her. "You'd be as scared as Chad was. I would be, too. Why weren't you scared, Abby?"

"I was. At first I thought Chad was tricking me again. Then I was so scared I couldn't move. And then after nothing terrible happened to me, I wasn't as scared."

Abby sipped Ovaltine as Ginny told a story about her great-aunt Minnie's umbrella being found hanging from the light chain upstairs in her grandmother's house. "Every time it was moved down to the umbrella stand in the hall, it would mysteriously appear on the light chain again."

It was fun to be at Nancy's house telling ghost stories. Nancy's mother invited her for lunch and called

Abby's mother for permission. They had tomato soup and toasted cheese sandwiches and Abby stayed until late in the afternoon, playing with Nancy's paper dolls and making up stories about them. Abby was glad Chad wasn't there to spoil things. On the way home she thought that now Nancy and Ginny were her friends, too, and she didn't feel as foreign in this snowy place so far from home.

TEN

*C*had was drinking milk at the table when Abby opened the kitchen door after hanging up her snow things.

"You're just going to have to put them right back on again," he said bossily.

"You can't make me." And he couldn't make her argue with him either. Abby changed the subject. "How'd you like getting pelted today?"

For an answer he burbled his milk at her.

"It wasn't fun, was it?"

He took his mouth out of the glass. He had a milk mustache and goatee, and a milk bubble hung from his nose. "It wasn't fair," he complained, "three against one."

"It wasn't fair for you to pelt me. You can throw better than I can," she said.

"It's not my fault you can't throw." His hair fell over one eye as he made a face and held the glass with his teeth.

"You look like a goat. You act like one, too. But goats don't know any better. You do."

Abby thought he was going to throw the glass at her, but instead he gulped the milk down as Aunt Noreen bustled in.

"Oh, Abby, I'm glad you're back. Don't gulp your milk, Chad. And comb your hair."

"Aw, Ma," he protested, "my cap'll mess it up again."

"Comb it, Chad." Aunt Noreen put a mound of butter, cheese, and a bottle of milk into a string bag. "Abby, I need you to go on an errand for me before it gets dark. Chad is going to take some things to the Elsters. They're patients of Thomas's who are always giving us vegetables from their garden. I want to send them some Christmas treats and a sledful of wood and coal for a cozy Christmas fire. Chad can manage the sled, but you'll have to carry the rest."

Behind Aunt Noreen's back Chad made a face again with an I-told-you-so grin and went to put on his boots. He didn't comb his hair.

"All right, Aunt Noreen," Abby said, dreading going anywhere with Chad. "But why can't you take them in the car?"

"The snow has drifted so high the road to their house is blocked, and I don't know when it will be passable. But you can go along the river path. Chad knows the way."

Abby put on her snow things again. When she lived in Florida, she had never realized how much trouble it was to put on and take off all those snow clothes. She pulled on her hat and wound the long scarf around her neck. At home she had hardly ever worn wool.

Chad had tied a load of wood from the woodshed and a sack of coal from the cellar to his sled. Aunt Noreen brought out the shopping bag. "Be careful with these, Abby. There's a box of candy and a little glass poodle for Mrs. Elster."

Chad was already halfway down the hill to the river. Abby struggled to catch up, afraid that if she tripped, she would tumble down into the ice-rimmed dark water and go over the falls. She didn't want to ask Chad to wait for her, so she trailed behind him down the path beside the noisy falls then up the hill to the Elsters'.

The white two-story farmhouse was warm and cozy inside with a big oil heater in a corner of the kitchen. Mrs. Elster's short white hair was arranged in finger waves. She wore a red-checked bib apron over her blue dress, and her face was pink from cooking. Mr. Elster had white hair, too, and white whiskers in his ears. He was tall and thin under his blue plaid flannel shirt and blue pants held up by suspenders. Chad introduced Abby as his cousin from Florida. They sat at the kitchen table as Mrs. Elster bustled around, making them hot Ovaltine. Mr. Elster asked Abby to put the presents under a tiny tree made from evergreen branches in the middle of the table.

Aunt Noreen's two green and red boxes joined several lumpy packages tied with lopsided bows that Mr. Elster said were from the grands. Abby admired the tree decorated with tiny painted wooden birds perched in the tree's branches or nestled in little straw nests.

"I carved them from peach seeds," Mr. Elster said. "Effie made the nests out of straw."

"Chad's making a house out of wooden matchsticks," Abby said, ignoring his frown. "It's for the twins, but he doesn't have enough used matches to finish it."

"Is that so?" Mr. Elster said, reaching for a box on a high shelf. "Happens I got plenty of used matchsticks. Never throw them away. You never know when you might have a use for them." He handed the box to Chad. It was full of more used matchsticks than Chad

had already put into the house. Now he could finish the house before Christmas. She would have to hurry to make the furniture.

Mrs. Elster set two steaming mugs in front of Abby and Chad and sat down. "Florida! My, my. You're a long way from home. How do you like Stratton Falls?"

"It's a lot different," Abby said.

"And you, young man. How do you like living in the Stratton House?"

"Stratton House?" Abby said.

"Why, yes, that's the name. It was built by the Stratton family. They were early settlers around here. That's why the town and river and falls are called that."

Maybe the Elsters would know something about the ghost. "Nancy says the house is haunted by a little girl at Christmastime," Abby said.

"Oh my, yes," Mrs. Elster said. "Lots of houses around here are said to be haunted. That house sure has a story."

"Oh, tell it to us, please," Abby said.

"The Strattons were long gone by the time I was born, but my mother knew the family," Mrs. Elster said. "She went to parties at the Strattons' house when she was a girl."

"When was that?" Abby prompted.

"Let me see. My mother was born in 1852 and was about the same age as the Stratton girl. What was her name? Phyllis? Phoebe? Something like that. Felicity. Felice. I remember now. It was Felicia, spelled with an *F.* Felicia Stratton. 'Course, the Strattons had a lot more money than my grandparents. O'Malley, they were. My mother told me Felicia's father—William his name was—sent her a red velvet dress from New York City. Told her he wanted her to wear it for him when he came home on furlough at Christmas. He was in the army then, on his way to Virginia. Anyway, it was during the Civil War, about 1864, I think."

"Did she wear it for him that Christmas?" Abby asked, suddenly anxious, as if she knew something had gone wrong.

"He didn't come home that Christmas." Mrs. Elster paused. Abby glanced at Chad. He was staring at Mrs. Elster. Maybe now he believed the ghost was real, Abby thought.

Mr. Elster got up to pour more Ovaltine in their mugs. Abby waited for the story to continue. "What happened then?"

"Oh, well, Felicia wore the red dress anyway. Velvet or velveteen, I believe it was. Very dear during the war, when manufacturers were making uniforms. But the Strattons were wealthy. They owned the mill and most of the land around here. Felicia wouldn't take the dress off when she went skating on the frozen river on Christmas Day. She had promised her dad she would wear it for him. My mother was there that day. She didn't have any skates, but she watched the others and saw it happen, Felicia with her long blonde hair wearing that red dress against the blue-white ice and snow. My mother wished she had such a beautiful dress. They played Crack the Whip. Felicia was on the end and couldn't hold on. The momentum threw her out near the middle of the river where the ice was thinnest. She just fell right through the ice. Nobody could get close enough to get her out. She came up two or three times and then disappeared. She must have gone over the falls, because she was never found."

"What—what happened to her father?" Abby asked. She knew what Felicia looked like with her long blonde hair. The red dress wasn't velveteen. It was rich velvet, the color of blood. "Did he ever come back?"

"Oh, yes, he came back. He was wounded in a battle somewhere in Tennessee—Franklin, I think it was—and nursed by a family of Union sympathizers who hid him from Confederate patrols. He didn't come back until the end of the war. My mother said he was so brokenhearted over Felicia that he refused to set foot in the house again. The family moved out west—California, I think. Some folks say Felicia still walks in that dress at Christmastime so her father will come back."

"I heard the ghost appears when somebody is about to die," Mr. Elster began, but his wife interrupted him.

"Hush now, Henry, that's just some fancying up. Folks always say that about a ghost. If Felicia appears, I think it's because she wants her daddy to come back."

Was the ghost walking because Abby's daddy was going to die? Or already dead? An icy terror seized Abby's heart.

Mr. Elster plucked a tiny nest with a bluebird sitting in it. "Here, young 'un," he said to Abby. "Don't reckon you want any used wooden matches, so here's a bird for you. Bluebirds mean good luck. You can put it on your Christmas tree in Florida someday and remember old Mr. Elster in snowy New York!"

Abby found her voice. "Thank you. I will. And thank you for the Ovaltine," she said as she pushed back her chair. Chad got up, too, and thanked the Elsters.

"A pleasure," Mr. Elster said. "Wrap up warmly now, it's about dark out there and getting colder. I expect it's down near to zero already."

"Here's a little something for the doctor." Mrs. Elster gave Chad a package from the pantry. "Now don't be strangers," she called to them from the door.

Chad picked up the sled rope, and they followed their footprints back to the river path. The sky was dark and the wind had risen. The cold cut sharply through Abby's woolen clothes. She wanted to ask Chad what he thought about Mrs. Elster's story, but it was too cold to talk.

Abby worried over Mr. Elster's words. Was her father in danger? Or was it her mother with her headaches? Was that why Felicia was walking? To warn her? Abby couldn't stop worrying about her parents. The doctor said her mother's headaches were migraines caused by worry and stress over her missing husband. They were painful but not fatal. So Abby's father must be the reason Felicia was walking. He was in danger. She would ask Felicia. Maybe she would give Abby a sign.

But what could she do if it was true? Abby couldn't save her father far away in Europe. She didn't even know what country he was in or if he was safe in some kind of shelter in this awful cold winter. She was afraid he didn't have a house to stay in, maybe only a tent. Or maybe nothing at all, a bombed farmhouse, a drafty barn. She hoped the barn had straw he could burrow into away from the wind to keep warm.

They climbed the path beside the falls, frozen on the sides but with a torrent of water spilling over its lip in the middle. Now Abby got a good look at them as spray blew into her face. The river dropped about twenty feet from above, churning over big rocks at the bottom. She shuddered, thinking about Felicia going over them eighty years earlier.

Wind seemed to push them backward, and Abby slipped on a patch of smooth ice. Chad linked his free arm through hers and they leaned into the wind. She wondered if he was thinking about Felicia.

"Thanks for getting me the matchsticks," he mouthed in her ear as the wind tried to snatch his words. Climbing up beside the falls, they held on to each other, and she felt warmer. She slipped her other mittened hand into her pocket and felt Mr. Elster's little bird in its nest.

A bluebird for good luck.

ELEVEN

*A*fter supper, Abby tried to talk to Chad about Mrs. Elster's story, but he wouldn't listen. "I got things to do," he said bolting up the stairs with the box of matchsticks.

Tomorrow was Christmas Eve. He didn't have much time left to finish the house. Abby had to work on the furniture if she wanted to furnish the house. Aunt Noreen gave her all the scraps and buttons she needed.

Abby bumped into Chad in the upstairs hall as she went to her room, but he didn't even notice the scraps. She closed the door and set to work upholstering a cardboard sofa with red velvet.

McNab pushed open her door. His beady eyes watched her through his tangled hair.

"Go away, McNab," she said, shoving him with cardboard.

He ignored her and crawled under her bed. Abby forgot about him as she cut and folded and glued and sewed. For a time she forgot to worry about her father as she concentrated on furnishing the matchstick house.

Abby didn't know how many rooms Chad had divided the house into and she didn't want to arouse his suspicions by asking. She planned to make furniture for a living room, dining room, bedroom, and kitchen. The stove was easy, a white box with round black burners and dials drawn on. Four small cardboard pillboxes glued together made a chest with push-out drawers. She made a skirted dresser with a pocket mirror to hang over it. Two spools and a rectangle of cardboard covered with cloth made a dining table with button plates. Abby planned to make a tree at the last minute by sticking the tip of an evergreen branch into a spool and hanging tiny decorative buttons on it for ornaments. She made lamps out of more spools and fluted candy cups from an empty box and set them on larger up-ended pillboxes.

Hours passed and Abby almost forgot her mission. But when the downstairs clock struck eleven, she went to Chad's room and knocked below the KEEP OUT—THIS MEANS YOU sign.

"Who is it?"

"Abby."

"What do you want?"

"To come in."

"What for?"

"To ask you something."

"Oh, all right."

He unlocked the door and went back to his bed, where he was gluing matchsticks.

"Do you believe we saw Felicia's ghost last night?" she asked as he stuck on another matchstick.

"No," he said without looking up. "I didn't see anything and I don't believe you did either."

"I did. I described her to you. She looked just like what Mrs. Elster said Felicia looked like. How could I know that if I didn't see her?" she reasoned.

"Nancy told you she was wearing a red velvet dress."

That was true. "But she didn't tell me it was an old-fashioned dress or that the ghost was wearing high-buttoned shoes from the nineteenth century."

"I didn't see any of that and you didn't either," he said stubbornly.

"Let's go see if she comes again," Abby coaxed.

"No. It's a waste of time. There's no such thing as ghosts. People just say that because of what happened to that girl."

"Felicia. Felicia Stratton. She was a real girl and she

lived in this house. Walked on these floors, ate in the dining room. Slept here, maybe in this very room."

"Stop it! This was not her room. And she isn't a ghost. It's a made-up story and you didn't see anything!"

Abby stared at him. Chad really was scared. "All right, I'll go by myself."

"No. Don't go down there."

"I have to."

"It's your funeral," he said, chopping off a match head.

She closed the door behind her and went down the stairs. Aunt Noreen had left the hall light on. Abby turned it off. She would rely on the upstairs light to be sure the house was dark enough for the ghost.

The clock ticked loudly in its corner. Abby sat on the stairs to wait. She had left McNab in her room. Now she wished she had his growly presence to keep her company.

She wondered what Chad was doing. She had forgotten to notice how many rooms were in the matchstick house. She tried to remember how many dining chairs she had already made and how many lamps. And how was she going to make a kitchen sink? Maybe she could cut a rectangle in a box and glue a smaller box lid in it for a sink. Snaps and a hook from the sewing box would make the tap and faucets.

Maybe the ghost wasn't coming. It was already past the time she had come before. Abby whispered her name. "Felicia. Felicia." She didn't want to think of Felicia as a ghost. She had been a real girl once, a girl just about Abby's age.

Someone was at the front door. Abby listened for the knock, but it didn't come. Maybe it was Uncle Thomas. She waited for the jingle of his keys in the lock. He wouldn't come to the front door. It was far from the garage. He would come in the back way, not the front.

The lock was silent and the door didn't open. But someone was there. Abby peered through the dim hall. Dots of light seemed to vibrate and coalesce into a shape, and then Abby saw Felicia. She walked erectly, eyes straight ahead, slowly through the hall to the parlor entrance. She seemed to glide, but her feet in the old-fashioned boots made wet footprints on the slate flooring. She crossed the dark Oriental carpet and passed through the Christmas tree in the middle of the parlor. Then Abby remembered. Felicia hadn't opened the front door. She had walked through it.

Abby followed the wet footsteps around the tree. On the other side Felicia sat on the sofa as before, hands in her lap, her eyes cast down.

"I . . . uh . . . I . . ." Abby's voice came out in a croak. She was talking to a ghost. "I know your story,

Felicia," she said in a whisper. "Your father came back safely from the war. He was wounded, but a Union family hid him and nursed him back to health. He came home at the end of the war. That was in 1865, I think."

The ghost raised her head. She looked into Abby's eyes but didn't seem to see her. She didn't seem to see anything. She seemed to be looking through Abby.

"He was safe," Abby said again. But the ghost stared through Abby, through the Christmas tree. She couldn't see either of them. She could only see what was there in 1864, Abby thought. If the Strattons had had a Christmas tree then, it must not have been in the middle of the parlor.

Abby repeated what Mrs. Elster had said about Mr. Stratton. But Felicia didn't hear. She began to fade, first her boots, her hands, her dress, and then her face. Her eyes were the last to disappear. They lingered in the dark, luminous and sad.

Abby walked over to the Christmas tree. She took Mr. Elster's nested bluebird from her pocket and hid it on the inside of a branch high up on the Christmas tree.

For luck.

TWELVE

*C*hristmas Eve had always been the most thrilling day of the year, a day filled with expectation, last-minute shopping, baking, wrapping presents. Abby tried not to think about Christmases past. She looked out the window and saw that more snow had fallen during the night. The river had frozen over and was white now all the way across.

It was too early to get up, the sun was not yet over the horizon, but she couldn't go back to sleep. She got her box of scraps and burrowed under the covers to work on the dollhouse furniture. The furnace had not yet turned on, and the house was cold from the night. Abby made a kitchen sink and lined it with silver foil from a candy wrapper. The kitchen table was a circle of cardboard glued to a spool with a round red-and-white checked tablecloth over it. Bottle caps made pots and vases and trash cans. Abby wished she had some rugs for the house.

When she heard Aunt Noreen in the kitchen and Uncle Thomas leaving for the hospital, Abby got up. She dressed quickly and met her mother on the stairs. "Merry Christmas," she said, giving her mother a hug.

"You're supposed to say that tomorrow," Mom said, with a laugh.

"I know. But I felt like starting a day early. Mom, can you crochet a little rug real quick," Abby whispered.

"How big?"

Abby explained.

"Of course. I can do that in a jiffy. I'll start right after breakfast and bring it to your room when I finish."

Abby gave her another hug. Some problems could be solved, she thought. The little ones.

Downstairs Abby saw that the hall light was on. She reached to turn it off and noticed that the lamp sat on a round table protector. It was dark blue with red and gold flowers and green leaves. It looked just like a living room rug and was just the right size for the dollhouse. She went to the kitchen to ask Aunt Noreen if she had another one.

"Isn't there one in your room?" she asked, popping

bread in the toaster. "I try to keep them under all the lamps so they won't scratch the tabletops."

"I thought you might have an extra one."

Aunt Noreen rummaged in a drawer in the pantry and found another one. "This one was too small for the hall lamp. I saved it in case I bought another lamp. That was before the war, when people could still buy lamps."

"It's perfect," Abby said, and ran to her room, leaving her aunt looking mystified that a girl could get excited over a table protector. Abby giggled to herself. Aunt Noreen would be surprised tomorrow when she saw what it was for.

After breakfast Chad went back to his room. He only had today to finish the house and let the glue dry. Abby took the twins outside to make a snowman. Nancy and Ginny and Davy came over to help, and they made a group of snowpeople, redoing what was left of the snowChad. But none of them looked like Abby or Chad. They just looked like regular snowmen and snowwomen.

Abby brought the twins in at noon. They were excited because Santa Claus was coming tonight.

Polly hung her jacket up as Patty dumped snow out of her boot. "What's he bringing you?" Polly asked Abby.

Abby unwound her scarf. "I don't know."

"What didja ask for?" Patty asked.

"I didn't ask for anything."

"You didn't write a letter? We did. We wrote a letter together," Patty said. "Then we decided Santa might think we're just one. So we each wrote another one."

"But we asked for the same things," Polly said.

I only want one thing for Christmas, Abby thought. Well, two things. I want my daddy to be safe and I want him here with us. But she didn't tell the twins. It would make them sad, and she wanted them to be happy on Christmas. Because they were so bubbly and sweet, she couldn't help being happier around them.

"It's not too late," Patty said.

"You can wish on the Christmas tree," Polly said.

Each twin took one of her hands and led her into the parlor and up to the tree.

"Close your eyes," Patty said.

"Then make a wish," Polly said.

Abby closed her eyes and held their hands and wished, and because they were so sure, she almost believed herself that wishing on a Christmas tree could make a wish come true. And then she realized why Felicia came back at Christmastime. She could hardly wait to tell Chad.

He emerged from his room for lunch. When the twins ran off to play, Abby asked Chad if he'd finished the house.

He made a face. "Wouldn't you like to know?"

She would, but she decided to change the subject and tell him her news. "I know why Felicia comes back," she said. "She misses her family. She comes back hoping they will come, too. But they can't because they moved to California."

He gave her a scornful look. "That's stupid. If a ghost walks, it's because somebody is going to die. Like Mr. Elster said. Everybody knows that."

"That's not true," Abby said. "You didn't see her the way I did. She's lonesome and sad and misses her family. That's why she comes back."

"Is not."

"It is, it is, it is," Abby said, suddenly furious with Chad and his superior ways. "It is not because somebody is going to die. You think you know everything. You said there's no such thing as a ghost and we didn't see one, but we did. I did and you did, too. You were just too scared to admit it. I saw how your eyes bugged out and you almost strangled, you were so scared."

"I was not!" he yelled. He picked up a pot lid off the stove to throw at her.

The lid was hot and he burned his fingers. "Oooowww!" he yelped, sucking his fingers.

"Children! What is going on?" Aunt Noreen rushed into the kitchen with a red tablecloth over her shoulder, her hands full of red and green napkins. "Chad, what is the matter with your fingers?"

"She made me do it," he muttered, scowling furiously.

"Abby, what did you do?" Aunt Noreen turned to her, one dark eyebrow raised.

"I didn't do anything. He picked up that lid to throw at me and it was still hot. He burned his fingers."

"Is this true, Chad?"

"She called me a coward." He wouldn't look at Abby.

"Let me see your hand." Aunt Noreen examined Chad's fingers. "Looks normal to me. Put some cold water on it just in case. Or even better, snow. I think you two could use a good dose of snow shoveling to use up some of that energy. Put on your snow things and start on the front walk."

"But Aunt Noreen—" Abby began.

"No buts," Aunt Noreen said firmly. "Out, both of you."

Abby was outraged. She hadn't done anything to Chad and had spent the morning looking after the twins, and this was her reward. She brushed past Chad, pushing him backward so that he had to grab the table to keep from falling.

"I'll get you for this," he said under his breath.

"If I hear any arguing or see any fighting from either of you, you will both have supper in your rooms and go to bed without opening presents," Aunt Noreen called after them.

By the time they finished shoveling the walks, supper was almost ready. Chad's face was red from the exertion. "Your nose looks like a cherry," Abby said as they went through the kitchen after shedding their outdoor wear.

Polly heard her. "Chad has a Santa Claus nose," she said with delight.

"And Santa Claus cheeks!" Patty added, giggling. She puffed out her cheeks.

Polly poked out her stomach. "And a Santa Claus belly!"

Patty poked hers out, too. "Like a bowlful of jelly!"

Their Santa imitations soon made Abby laugh. Even Chad had to grin as they went to get ready for supper.

"Ho ho ho!" Uncle Thomas boomed in the hall, ringing a dinner bell.

The dining room was festive with swags of evergreen, tied with red and green bows hung from the corners of the room to the light fixture over the table. A pyramid of fruit with greenery tucked into it sat in the center of the table. The twins were almost too excited to eat, but Uncle Thomas told them they had to finish so they would have enough strength to open their presents. Abby thought the food was wonderful—baked ham, Boston baked beans, applesauce, a jar of Mrs. Elster's pickled peaches and other kinds of pickles, hot bread with real butter, and fruitcake for dessert.

"I'm too full to open presents," Uncle Thomas declared.

"Dad-dee," said the twins together.

"Don't worry," Chad told the twins. "He says that every year."

"He's just as excited as you two are," Abby's mother teased. "He was always the first one at the Christmas tree when we were growing up."

"He still is," Aunt Noreen said.

Everyone pitched in to clear the table. The twins were in agony, waiting for Abby to wash the dishes so they could dry them and Chad could put them away. "I'm hurrying as fast as I can," Abby said. "I don't want to break anything!"

But finally they all sat around the tree, children on the floor. Aunt Noreen and Abby's mother on the sofa. Uncle Thomas wore a red velvet Santa hat with a white pom-pom on the end that bobbed when he hohohoed. He was too tall and thin to look like Santa, but he had merry blue eyes. He put a record of Christmas carols on the Victrola and picked up a package with an enormous purple Santa card. "Hohoho. What do we have here? A present to Abby from Patty and Polly."

Abby carefully untied the red cord bow and unwrapped the package. Inside she found a black felt stuffed Scottie with a red plaid bow around its neck. "It looks just like McNab," she exclaimed, as though she were thrilled to have a replica of that awful dog. "Thank you. I'll call him McTab."

The twins giggled and opened their books from Abby next, then Chad opened the giant box of all kinds of candy from the twins. "Every kind there is," Patty told him.

"One of each from Denton's," Polly said. "Try them."

"Later," Chad said. "I'm still full from supper."

Uncle Thomas seemed pleased with his picture frame and took it to his office across the hall to put on his desk. Aunt Noreen thanked Abby for her handkerchief.

"It's from Ireland," Abby pointed out.

"Just the thing for a Noreen with two Irish grandmothers," she said.

Abby watched anxiously as Uncle Thomas handed the two presents from her to her mother.

"Why, Abby, what a surprise," she said, turning the box over and over. "Two presents. I'm overwhelmed."

She loved the scarf and knotted it around her neck. "It's beautiful," she said, stroking the soft green folds.

She opened the box and sat for a minute looking at the pearls with the card Abby had made explaining that they were really from Dad. Her eyes were misty as she hugged Abby. "I feel like a queen," she said, and asked Abby to fasten the pearls around her neck over the scarf.

Uncle Thomas handed Abby a present from Chad. She was almost afraid to open it. It was probably some kind of trap to pinch her fingers or something slimy and horrible. She picked up the red-wrapped present. It felt like a book. But that could be a disguise. Cautiously, she removed the paper and found a book—Louisa May Alcott's *Eight Cousins*, which she hadn't read. Abby wondered if Chad had bought it at the used-book store. He had probably picked it because he thought she wouldn't like a book about a girl with eight boy cousins. He probably thought she thought one boy cousin was enough. He was right. But she thanked him.

Chad opened Abby's present. "*Penrod and Sam*, by Booth Tarkington. Thanks, Abby."

She couldn't tell if he liked it or not.

Chad's presents to the twins were the little dolls made of wood with painted-on hair and matching dresses, one in red and one in blue. Abby wondered when he planned to give them the matchstick house. If he brought it downstairs tonight, she would put the furniture in it after everybody was in bed.

"And now it's time to go to sleep so the real Santa Claus can make his visit," Uncle Thomas said.

This was one night in the year when nobody protested going to bed early. Abby was the first one up the stairs. Aunt Noreen had given her some old house magazines. She wanted to look through them to find pictures to put on the house walls. Her mother came to her room to tell her good night. "Here are the things you wanted," she said. She pulled two circles and an oval out of her pocket and handed them to Abby.

"Rugs!" Abby exclaimed as she examined the crocheted circles, a white one, a red and white one, and a dark blue oval. "You made all of these today?"

"It doesn't take long," she said.

"Thanks, Mom." Abby hugged her for a long time. She wished Daddy were here, and she knew her mother wished the same thing, but neither of them said it. Abby was afraid she would cry. "Sleep tight," her mother whispered.

The house was soon quiet. Abby snipped pictures of flowers, birds, and fruit from the magazines. Several times she thought she heard noises downstairs. Once somebody said, "Shhhh." And another time something bumped a wall, but that was probably Uncle Thomas coming upstairs. At ten-thirty the house was quiet. Abby gathered the furnishings and glue.

The hall lamp was on, and Abby left it for now. Felicia wouldn't come for another hour. Abby plugged in the tree lights so she could see what she was doing and began to furnish the house. Chad had placed it in front of the tree so the twins couldn't miss it in the morning. Abby glued the curtains on the windows and the pictures on the walls first. Then she arranged the furniture. The house had four rooms, just as she had expected, two on each floor. She put the red and white rug in the kitchen in front of the sink. The blue rug went in the dining room under the table, the white rug in the bedroom. Abby put the flowered table protector in the living room, where it made an elegant rug. She had fashioned a cardboard fireplace with fire cut from a house magazine. She glued two little red velvet stockings to its mantel so they seemed to be hanging there. She was so busy, she hardly noticed when the clock struck eleven.

When she was done, she unplugged the tree lights and turned off the hall lamp. Then she sat down in the window seat to wait. With the parlor dark, she opened the blackout curtains onto the bright snowscape. The snowpeople they'd made this morning stood on the left. The hill sloped down to the frozen river. Abby watched for Felicia.

The house was silent, sleeping. Suddenly Abby became aware that someone was in the room. She turned away from the window and saw Felicia entering from the hall. For a moment she disappeared in the tree, then reemerged from its boughs. Abby felt the hair on the back of her neck tingle, even though she had known it would happen.

Felicia sat down on the sofa and put her hands in her lap. Abby stood by the tree where she could see Felicia's face. "Hello, Felicia," she said softly.

Felicia raised her eyes just as she had before and stared past or through Abby.

"Your father came home from the war," Abby repeated. "But he was so sad about you that he moved to California."

As she finished speaking, she realized that something was different. She glanced at Felicia's face and saw that Felicia's blue eyes were looking straight into hers.

Felicia was watching her!

THIRTEEN

*F*elicia?" Abby said softly.

The ghost didn't answer. Her eyes blinked and filled with sadness as she looked into Abby's eyes across eighty years of time. Felicia's lips parted.

"What is it?" Abby prompted.

But Felicia didn't reply. Her lips closed as she glanced around, searching for familiar faces and objects, her eyes lingering on the tree, the mantel, the window seat, as if she were seeing the 1944 room for the first time.

"Why do you come back, Felicia? Is it because you miss your family?" Abby persisted.

Again, no answer. Felicia's eyes moved over the room.

"Are you waiting for your father to come back from the war? Is that why you come here every night in the red dress?"

Felicia did not move or reply. Her eyes strayed past Abby, still searching for something familiar from her time.

"It's 1944 now, Felicia, not 1864. In 1865 your father came back safely from the war. Your family moved to California. That's why you can't find them. They aren't here."

As Abby spoke, tears glistened in Felicia's eyes, but she didn't seem surprised. Maybe she knew they weren't here.

"Is it . . ." Abby faltered. She didn't think she could get the words out, but she had to know. "Is it my father? Do you come back to warn me of—of danger to him?"

Felicia didn't answer. She stared directly at Abby now. Tears spilled from her eyes and slid down her cheeks. In the shadowy light they made silvery trails on her face and sparkled as they splashed on her hands, on the sleeves of her dress, on her red velvet lap.

"Is there anything I can do to help him?" Abby asked.

But Felicia had begun to fade slowly.

"Wait! Don't go," Abby begged.

Felicia's feet dissolved into small bright dots, then her hands, her dress, her face, her eyes until only the glittering motes of her tears hung like dangling crystals in the air, and in a moment they, too, were gone.

"No!" Abby said fiercely aloud, "I won't let anything happen to him. It can't. Not my father." But the room was empty. She looked down at her fists clenched in her lap.

He's not going to die, he's not, he's not, he's not, Abby chanted until she fell asleep.

"It's Christmas!" Polly yelled in the hall outside Abby's door.

"Wake up, everybody!" Patty yelled.

"Hohoho," Polly sang in a deep Santa voice.

Abby hurriedly put on her robe and slippers and poked her head out of the door as Patty jingled a bunch of bells.

"Merry Christmas, Abby!" the twins said together. They wore clusters of holly in their tousled hair and looked like a pair of Christmas elves in their footed green pajamas.

"Beat you downstairs!" Chad shouted, bursting out of his room on the run.

Abby and the twins rushed ahead of him, but Chad slid down the banister, hitting the newel post at the bottom with a hard thunk. "I beat!" he smirked.

"No fair," Polly said.

"You cheated," Patty said.

Chad ran into the parlor. "All's fair in the Christmas morning race. Look what Santa brought!"

"A little house!" squealed Patty.

"A dollhouse," squeaked Polly, "with furniture in it."

"Furniture?" Chad had a funny look as he knelt to look.

Abby pretended she had never seen the furniture before as the twins exclaimed over the mirror, the bottle cap pie plate with its crisscross of clay pastry, the tablecloth, the bed pillows, the pictures.

"Look," Patty said, "it's got real rugs!"

"And curtains!" Polly said.

The grown-ups arrived and admired the house and its miniature contents. Aunt Noreen put a record of Christmas carols on the Victrola, and Uncle Thomas plugged in the tree lights. "What else did Santa bring?" he asked.

Santa had brought Chad a red sweater, a Monopoly game, two Hardy Boys books, a chemistry set, a microscope set, and a wooden chess set. For the twins, he'd brought green velvet jumpers; new dolls, each with a cardboard trunk of doll clothes, and wooden doll beds; new tea sets, one with red flowers and one with blue ones; and Chinese checkers.

On her side of the tree Abby found a new red wool coat, two Nancy Drew mysteries, fuzzy white mittens, watercolor paints, and a pad. But best of all was the red velvet dress, its skirt spread beneath the tree. She touched the soft velvet sleeve. This was what her mother had been doing up in her room all those times, making Abby's present. The dress was old-fashioned with a V neck and white lace collar that came to points. The long sleeves ended in white lace cuffs. The waist was dropped and fitted with a gathered skirt attached to it. It was the prettiest dress she'd ever had.

Their stockings were filled with fruit, nuts, chocolate, and candy canes. Even McNab had a stocking with a big dog biscuit shaped like a bone sticking out of it.

In a red-checked apron, Uncle Thomas made his specialty, applesauce pancakes, flipping them with a flourish. Then everybody pitched in to help prepare Christmas dinner. Abby peeled potatoes while Chad peeled onions. He made a big show of sobbing as he did it, making the twins laugh.

"If you kept your mouth closed, the onions wouldn't make you cry," his mother told him as she stirred a pot of beans.

Chad only sobbed louder, and Aunt Noreen said, "There's a lot of ham in those onions."

Christmas dinner was ready at two o'clock. Uncle Thomas announced it by ringing the bell. "Hear ye, hear ye, it is now time for Christmas dinner."

Abby put on her new dress and the twins put on their jumpers and white blouses. Chad pulled his new red sweater on over his blue shirt. Uncle Thomas wore a red-and-green plaid tie. Aunt Noreen's dress was red wool, and Abby's mother wore a green dress and the string of Christmas pearls. The twins tied a red bow on McNab. He sat under the table near Abby, waiting for tidbits.

"We are certainly a Christmassy-looking family," Uncle Thomas observed as they waited for him to carve the turkey.

But first they held hands and everybody said what they were thankful for or wished for.

"I'm thankful for another Christmas. I hope this war will end soon," Uncle Thomas said, "and John will be with us again."

"I hope he is safe and well," Abby's mother said almost in a whisper.

When Abby's turn came, she missed her daddy so much that her throat closed up. There was a long pause as she struggled to make the words come out.

Aunt Noreen said out of turn, "I'm thankful that Abby and Ellen could be here with us."

Abby found her voice. "I wish my daddy was here and I hope he gets his Christmas package."

Chad said he wished everybody's wishes would

come true. The twins wished for Abby's daddy to come back.

For a minute Abby thought her mom was going to cry, and if she did, Abby knew she would cry, too. She didn't want to cry on Christmas Day and spoil it for the twins and everyone. She blinked hard and held her breath to stop the tears.

Quickly Uncle Thomas asked her mother to help him with the plates, and the moment passed.

"Abby, you are a picture in that dress," Aunt Noreen said, spooning dressing. "I wish I could take color pictures of our Christmas family."

"Abby's dress looks like the one in the story Nancy told Davy," Patty said.

"The Christmas ghost story," Polly said as she dipped the spoon into the bowl of creamed onions. "Davy told us."

"That doesn't sound very merry," Aunt Noreen warned.

Uncle Thomas changed the subject. "Who needs potatoes?"

He passed the bowl to Abby. She took it automatically. Her thoughts were spinning with a flash of insight. Now she knew for sure why Felicia had come back. Now she knew what Felicia was trying to tell her. It was the dress.

That had been Felicia's message all along. She wanted Abby to wear the red dress on Christmas Day so her father would come home safely, as Felicia's had in that other war.

An icicle ran down Abby's back as she remembered that Felicia hadn't been here when her father came home because she had been lost in the river. But that wouldn't happen to Abby. She was safe because she had been warned. She knew Felicia's story. She wouldn't go ice-skating on the river or anywhere else. She didn't know how to ice-skate. She wouldn't go on the ice, or play Crack the Whip on it.

Suddenly, for the first time in months, Abby stopped worrying about her daddy. He would be safe. Felicia had told her what to do. Now everything would be all right. Abby breathed a sigh of relief and settled down to eat her Christmas dinner.

FOURTEEN

*Y*ou're excused from doing the dishes," Aunt Noreen said as the grown-ups sat talking over coffee at the table. "Go enjoy Christmas."

Abby felt stuffed and sleepy, but she sat on the floor by the Christmas tree with the twins while they played with their dollhouse. They named their dolls Clementine and Christabel and said they were twins. McNab strolled over and climbed into her lap. Abby froze as he made his usual disagreeable noises.

"Why is he doing this?" she whispered to the twins.

"He likes you," Polly said.

"No, he doesn't. He snarls and growls at me all the time and shows his teeth."

"He only sits with people he likes," Patty said.

"So he must like you," Polly said.

Abby didn't think McNab really liked her. It was probably all the food she had given him.

McNab let out a loud snore. Abby sat still, careful not to wake him up. She wasn't sure the twins were right. Soon her legs began to feel stiff. She was glad when a knock on the front door roused him. He jumped out of her lap and ran to the front door to see who was there. Nancy and Ginny were bundled up and ready to go sledding. They had brought presents for Chad and Abby. Abby hadn't bought anything for them, but Aunt Noreen produced two packages, which held little painted wooden pins—a spotted puppy for Nancy and a white kitten for Ginny. They had gone in together to give Abby another Nancy Drew that she didn't have and a model-plane kit for Chad.

Chad and the twins ran to change into outdoor clothes, but Abby refused. When they asked her why, she could only say that the dress was her Christmas present and she wanted to wear it all day.

She couldn't tell them that to keep her daddy safe she had to wear the red dress on Christmas Day, the way Felicia had. They might try to stop her. So she was left with the grown-ups while the others went out to play. McNab crawled back into her lap.

"McNab has been sleeping too much lately. I think he needs some exercise," Aunt Noreen said. "Abby, how about taking him for a walk in the snow?"

"I guess I could do that." She wouldn't have to change, not just for a walk. Abby slipped on her boots while Uncle Thomas found McNab's leash and snapped it on—"to keep him from running in front of the sleds."

The sky was a bank of thick gray clouds. At home the sun would be blazing like summertime unless it was raining. Abby shivered in the velvet dress under Chad's old jacket. She stamped her feet to keep warm as McNab pulled on the leash and barked at the twins zipping down the hill on their sleds, followed by Nancy and Ginny with Davy.

"Sit, McNab," Abby ordered. McNab obeyed, sinking down into a little hollow in the snow.

"Look at that," Abby said in amazement, but Chad ignored McNab. "You made that furniture," he said when the others were far enough down the hill that they couldn't hear.

"Oh? What makes you think that?" Abby said, not giving anything away.

"I figured it out. It wasn't hard. Mom didn't do it. And I don't think Aunt Ellen did. I don't think she even knew about the house. But you did. So you had to be the one. I would've got furniture when I could've."

Abby concentrated on unwrapping the leash from her wrist. Should she admit it? It was fun having a secret from Chad. "It could have been the ghost," she teased.

He almost made a face and gave her a pained look. "There wasn't any ghost. You just made that up. And anyway, a ghost wouldn't make doll furniture."

"How do you know?"

"Because that's not what ghosts do. It was you, and I don't know why you won't admit it."

Abby relented. "But I didn't make the rugs. Mom did."

"Thanks." He said it like he was giving away rubies. He leaned over and brushed snow off his sled.

"I did it for the twins," Abby said. And because she was sorry she had almost spoiled the house. "It was fun."

"Here." Abruptly Chad held out the rope to his sled. "Want to take a turn?"

He looked down at the snow, but Abby knew he was watching her. Abby wasn't dressed for sledding. The red velvet skirt hung below her coat, but she had to show him she wasn't a scaredy-cat. Once down the hill wouldn't hurt if she was careful. Her coat covered most of her dress.

"Okay. Hold McNab for me."

Abby took the rope, lay down on her stomach, and pushed off. The sled shot down the run. It seemed that she was going faster than the last time, but she didn't drag her feet. She was afraid to go this fast but she wouldn't slow the sled, not this time. She wouldn't give Chad a chance to call her scaredy-cat again.

Freezing air pushed against Abby's face as the sled raced down the run, whipping her hair, stinging her eyes and cheeks, taking her breath away. The twins flashed by and then Nancy and Ginny and Davy as they pulled their sleds back to the top of the hill. Nancy yelled something, but her words were blown away by the sled's speed.

The hill was a blur of white. The sled was going faster than last time. It was almost as though something unseen had taken hold of it and propelled it faster than the other sleds. Abby didn't have time to wonder why. She had almost reached the bottom of the hill. She would have to stop soon.

But she held off a little longer. She was determined that nobody was going to laugh at her or call her scaredy-cat or 'fraidy-cat this time.

The bottom of the hill rushed toward her. It was time to stop the sled now. Abby dropped her feet into the snow, but instead of slowing down, the sled seemed to gather momentum. She tried to dig her toes in, but it was too late. Her feet skimmed helplessly behind the sled as it sped over the last few feet of the hill.

With a lurch the sled reached the end of the snow and skidded onto the frozen river. Abby couldn't stop it. She kicked and grabbed at branches, but she was going too fast.

The sled picked up speed on the ice. Abby leaned left to turn it back to the bank, but the ice was in control now and nothing she did made any difference. The sled headed out into the freshly frozen ice in the middle of the river.

The ice made groaning noises as the sled shot across it. The river had been frozen all the way across less than a day, but Abby couldn't think about that. She had only a fraction of a second to make a decision. She couldn't stop the sled, but maybe if she could get off, she wouldn't slide any farther. Abby rolled off the sled.

It didn't work. The sled kept going and so did Abby, but they weren't together now. The opposite bank came closer as she slid toward it. She tried to keep her chin up off the ice while she splayed her arms and legs out to stop herself.

Abby spun in a wide spiral, but before she came to a stop, the ice made a horrible cracking sound and moved beneath her. Now she could see the hill she had just come down, the faces of the twins and Chad and

Nancy and Ginny and Davy. Their mouths seemed to be open, as if they were yelling at her to stop. As if she could.

The ice cracked again and she came to an abrupt stop. The sky tilted crazily and water rose over the edge of the fissure. It sloshed over Abby, and she slid into the dark river below the ice.

FIFTEEN

*T*he water was shockingly cold, like liquid ice. Abby couldn't breathe. Her lungs seemed to be paralyzed. Her head went under, but she flailed with her arms until her face broke the surface and she was in air again. She choked on the water she had swallowed and tried to take several breaths, but each one felt like an icicle stabbing her lungs. She moved her feet to tread water until she could figure out how to get back onto the ice. As she surveyed her position, she saw that she was in a small pool of dark water surrounded by thin ice in the middle of the Stratton River.

Abby tried to hold on to the edge of the ice as she prepared to hoist herself onto it, but the water seemed to pull her down. Chunks of the ice broke off in her hands, and she plunged backward.

Water went up her nose, but she managed to keep her face afloat as she tried to analyze her situation. Abby could only think of three things to do: continue to tread water or hold on to the edge of the ice until somebody could rescue her or try to climb back up onto the ice by herself.

She couldn't wait for rescue. She had to try to save herself. Abby gathered her energy. She hurled herself upward again in a desperate attempt to throw herself onto the ice. But her body seemed too heavy to lift out of the water. She grabbed at the ice as chunk after chunk broke off, sending her deeper into the water each time. Her voice seemed frozen and no sound came out of her mouth. Why was the ice breaking like that? Why couldn't she fling herself up on it and crawl to safety?

Why didn't the others come to help her? What was taking them so long? Abby tried to hold her head above the water, to breathe air until they could help her. Her feet felt heavy, as though they were encased in cement. They wouldn't move no matter how hard she tried. Now she couldn't even tread water.

On the hill above the river, Chad jumped on Nancy's sled and sped down the hill with Nancy and Ginny on the other sled. The twins followed on their sled, and Davy and McNab raced alongside to keep up. They all seemed to be yelling and screaming, their faces frantic as their mouths opened and closed, but Abby couldn't hear them. She couldn't hear anything except the sounds of the water gurgling in her ears, pushing against her sodden clothes.

Abby sank down into the water until it covered her ears. Something seemed to drag her down into the depths of the dark water, something more than her heavy velvet skirt. She tried to kick off her leaden snow boots. She reached down to pull them off, but her bulky clothes hampered her movements. All thoughts of getting out of the ice had left her. Now she struggled just to keep her head above the water.

Chad halted the sled in a spray of snow at the edge of the river. He jumped off and cautiously made his way out across the ice until it began to growl ominously, like a protesting animal.

"I can't get any closer without it breaking," he called.

Abby didn't hear him, but she understood. Nobody could come near her now. She was trapped alone in this ice hole. She would freeze. Or drown. Whichever came first.

She would sink to the bottom of the cold dark water. It wouldn't matter whether she had frozen or drowned because by then she would be both. Sometime she would probably go over the falls, but that wouldn't matter either because she wouldn't feel it. She would be dead, drowned like Felicia.

Would she be a ghost like Felicia, too? A ghost in a red velvet dress? Would they come back together at Christmastime to walk through the house, perhaps unseen for another century?

The others ran along the shore of the river, Nancy and Ginny in one direction, Davy and the twins in the other. Where were they going? Were they abandoning her or going for help? It wouldn't do any good. Nobody could help her now.

McNab, loosed from his leash, ran in circles on the ice as close to her as he could without falling in, barking furiously. Abby saw his mouth move. Chad's moved, too. She didn't try to listen. She couldn't hear them, and anyway, it didn't matter. Nothing mattered. Her world was reduced to the cold dark water almost at eye level, the unrelenting ice, and the indifferent sky.

She hardly noticed when Nancy and Ginny found a long limb under the snow and managed to free it. They dragged it to Chad, and the three of them pushed it, with McNab pulling it, across the ice to Abby.

"Grab hold of the limb," they shouted together.

This time Abby heard them and understood. They could pull her out if she could hold on to the limb. Abby was too tired and too cold. But she had to try. She put her hands up and touched the limb. She felt it against her mittened palms and tried to close her fingers around it, but they no longer worked.

"I c–c–can't," she whispered, certain that no sound came out of her mouth.

"You have to!" Nancy yelled.

"Grab it!" Chad said.

"Grab it! Grab it!" the twins echoed with Davy.

Abby reached, but again her hands could only touch the limb. Her fingers curved uselessly in the sodden mittens.

Chad pulled the limb back to the shore, away from Abby. She was too tired to wonder what he was doing. It hurt to breathe. Her lungs were freezing. He took off his scarf. Why was he doing that when it was so cold?

Suddenly Abby was flooded with warmth. The water wasn't cold. It was warm like the Atlantic Ocean at Jacksonville Beach. Maybe even warmer. She wouldn't drown in this water. Why was she struggling so hard against it? The water was pleasant. She could just lie back in it and rest awhile. It would melt the ice inside her. Then she could breathe again and find a way out of the river. The river would help her. It was like the ocean. Warm and friendly.

Abby stopped moving. She sank lower and lower until the water closed over her head.

And then she knew why Felicia had returned.

SIXTEEN

The Western Union messenger stopped in front of Abby's house. He smiled at her and said, "Everything is all right." He handed her a telegram. She opened it and read that her daddy was at the beach waiting for her.

And then they were at the beach, building a sand castle, her daddy in a blue bathing suit, her mother in a one-piece suit the color of honey, and Abby in a red one. The tide was coming in, splashing all over the sand castle. "It will go back out again and we can make a new sand castle," her daddy said. "Every time the tide washes it away, we can do that."

Waves foamed around Abby's ankles and tickled them. It made her laugh. She loved to go to the beach with her parents. This water was warm, not like that icy river water in New York that she had dreamed about. She was glad her daddy was here and not missing in a horrible war in Europe.

Abby relaxed in the soft warm water. She was safe, everything was all right, just the way her daddy said, and he was safe, too. She could sleep here forever, but her mother would probably wake her for school in a few minutes. She opened her eyes, expecting to see sunshine through the white dotted swiss curtains in her room.

Instead her eyes burned with cold, and Abby knew that New York hadn't been a dream. Florida was the dream. Her daddy was still lost somewhere in the war in Europe, and she was freezing and drowning in the Stratton River, weighted by the red velvet dress that was supposed to make her daddy safe and bring him home.

Just as Abby's eyes began to close for the last time, she saw something red looming above her in the blue-white blur of the ice and snow. She was too tired to care. She would sleep a little while.

A face floated above her, concerned blue eyes watched her as she dreamed about the girl in the red velvet dress. Not now, Abby tried to say, I'm too tired to play now.

A hand reached out to her, a hand at the end of a long red sleeve, a red velvet sleeve. Felicia!

Abby's eyes opened. Felicia knelt above her on the

edge of the ice. Her dress was the color of blood against the ice, snow, and sky. Something of the dress's vividness reached Abby as she watched Felicia's hand slide into the water above her head. With renewed energy, Abby kicked her feet in their waterlogged boots and pumped her arms. Her face broke the surface, and Felicia grasped her left hand. It felt warm to Abby, but she had learned that she couldn't trust warmth in this treacherous place. Nothing was as it seemed. The hand of a ghost girl was warmer than her own.

Frantically, Abby tried to beat at the water with her free hand. But her movements were slowed by the cold and her exhaustion. Again she slid down into the river and would have gone under, but Felicia's hand held her back.

"I'm cold," Abby said. "Let me go in the warm water."

Felicia tightened her grasp.

Chad was still playing with the scarf. He had tied it into a wide loop on the end of the limb. Why was he decorating that limb? He ignored Felicia and pushed the limb past her toward Abby. What was he doing now?

"Put your head in the loop!" he yelled.

He was trying to lasso her head with the scarf. This was no time for silly games. Did he think she was a cow?

Nancy and Ginny and Chad yelled at her. Abby couldn't hear what they were saying. The twins hopped around, Davy jumped up and down. McNab ran out on the ice and back to the bank, back and forth, back and forth, but closer than the others, barking as if to tell her something.

It was all terribly confusing. "Go away," she said. "I want to take a nap." Her mouth moved, but no sound came out. She was too tired and out of breath to speak again. She wanted to fall back into the waiting warmth of the water and rest awhile, but Felicia wouldn't let go of her hand.

"Let go," Abby said. "Let go."

"No," someone said softly.

"No, no, no," the voice repeated. "You must not go under the water again. If you do, you may never come back."

Abby tried to pull away, but Felicia held her hand tightly.

"Let me go," Abby whispered. "I need to rest, just for a minute."

Felicia's grip was unyielding. The only warmth Abby felt came from that hand. It was a lifeline, keeping her head above the water. If Felicia let go, Abby would sink down for the last time. And it would be forever, because she didn't have the strength or the will to surface again.

Chad dangled the scarf noose over Abby's head, then let it drop to her shoulders.

"Bull's-eye!" he shouted. "Now let it go under your arms."

Then Abby understood. He didn't think she was a cow. He was trying to rescue her. Abby managed to slip her right arm through the noose. She tried to lift her left hand, but her arm wouldn't move.

"It's not working," Ginny said.

"Keep trying, Abby," Nancy called.

Abby tried. But even with Felicia's help, she couldn't raise her arm again.

"Let's try another way," Chad said. They pulled the limb uphill in an attempt to drag Abby out of the water.

The noose began to slip.

"It's coming off!" Nancy yelled.

"Stop before it's all the way off," Ginny screamed.

The noose went slack again.

Don't give up, Abby thought, but she was too tired to say the words. There's always another way to do something. She wanted to tell them to analyze the situation.

Abby didn't have to analyze her situation now. She couldn't last much longer in the icy water. She had to get her left arm through the noose. It was her only chance, and she couldn't do it.

Her breath came in shallow gasps now and each one might be her last. How long did it take a person to freeze? She knew she was close, even with Felicia holding her hand.

"Try again, Abby, try to get your left arm in the noose again," Chad shouted.

Once more Abby tried to raise her left arm, but this time she couldn't even get it to the surface of the water. She was trapped in this ice hole. She couldn't get out, not ever. She would freeze here like Felicia had. She would be swept over the falls and disappear forever. She would become a ghost like Felicia. Abby closed her eyes as her head went under again.

"I can't," she whispered.

Abby felt her left arm lifting by itself. She opened her eyes and watched as Felicia tugged at her velvet sleeve, freeing it from the greedy river, lifting it into the noose.

"You're doing it!" Nancy yelled.

I'm not, Abby wanted to say. I can't move at all. It's Felicia. But she was too close to freezing to speak.

Felicia settled the noose under Abby's arms. She held Abby's hands and guided her as Chad and Nancy and Ginny and Davy and the twins pulled her across the ice to safety.

Felicia stood back and watched until Abby reached the safety of thick ice that could support her weight.

Felicia's velvet dress was blindingly red against the winter landscape. Abby would never forget the intensity of that red. Felicia seemed to hover over the ice for a moment, her eyes locked on Abby's, and then she was gone.

Abby closed her heavy eyelids. She was too tired to try to open them again. Maybe they were frozen shut.

" 'M iceAbby," she tried to say through chattering teeth.

"What?" somebody said. Abby thought it was Ginny.

" 'M iceAbby," she repeated.

"She said 'might be mice,' I think," somebody said.

"No, she said 'mice be,' " someone else said.

"Mice be what?"

"I think she's delirious," Chad said.

"Felicia," Abby said clearly, and this time Chad understood her.

SEVENTEEN

*T*hey stood her upright and bundled all their coats around her, then propelled her between them up the hill to the house. Abby couldn't feel her feet. She couldn't feel McNab when he ran between them. She stumbled and would have fallen backward down the hill if they hadn't been holding her, with the twins pushing from behind. Davy ran ahead to tell the grown-ups.

Their anxious faces met her on the hill. They brought her into the warm safety of the house.

" 'M okay," she told them, but they didn't seem to believe her. They put her into the bathtub filled with tepid water that they warmed slowly to steamy hot and then they poured in an entire bottle of pungent lavender salts. Abby thought she had been wet enough for one day and she was suspicious of water temperature now, but she began to feel normal again.

"Ah choo!" The salts tickled her nose.

"Thomas, she's caught a cold," Aunt Noreen said.

"It's the lavender," Abby protested, but they made her put on flannel pajamas and wool socks and get into bed with extra covers piled on top and a hot water bottle to hug. McNab settled himself on her feet, and Abby thought she had never been so warm.

They fussed over her, plumping up her pillows, tucking the covers around her. Her mother draped a shawl over her. Aunt Noreen rubbed her hair with a succession of towels warmed in front of the fire and raced upstairs by a relay of the twins and Davy until her hair was dry, and then she wrapped Abby's head in a warm dry towel and over that another wool shawl. "The head is where people catch cold," she explained to Abby. "That's why it's called a head cold."

Her mother sat on the bed and rubbed Abby's hands between her own long fingers until Abby's hands were warm again. She looked worried, with tiny vertical frown lines above her nose like little quotation marks.

"I'm fine," Abby assured her. "I didn't drown. I couldn't. Felicia was holding my hands." She told them how Felicia had saved her, but that alarmed them even more.

"Chad saw her," Abby explained. "He knows Felicia is real. Tell them, Chad."

Chad was called in from the hall.

"Chad, did you see this other girl Abby says was there helping with her rescue?" Aunt Noreen asked.

He shook his head. "I didn't see anybody but Abby in the river," he said, not meeting her eyes.

"Thomas, she's delirious," Aunt Noreen called.

Uncle Thomas had been in the background. Now he stuck a thermometer under her tongue and took her temperature. It was normal.

"I told you, I'm fine. Please let me get up," Abby begged. "I don't have a fever. Do I, Uncle Thomas?"

He admitted she didn't, but they made her stay in bed anyway. "Just to be on the safe side," Uncle Thomas said. But he wouldn't let them rub her chest with Musterole and said she didn't need cough syrup unless she started coughing.

Then she was alone in her room. Abby opened *The Secret of the Old Clock.* Someone knocked softly. "Come in."

Chad stuck his head into the room. "Can I come in?"

"I said come in, didn't I?"

"That was before you knew it was me." He looked so different with his hair plastered to his head, comb marks still visible.

"You just pulled me out of the freezing river and saved my life. Why wouldn't I want you to come in? Besides, it's boring in here by myself."

He didn't seem convinced. "Yeah, I know all that. But it was my fault you sledded into the river."

"How could it be your fault?"

"I waxed the runners of my sled to make it go faster."

Abby sat up on the pillows. "So that was why the sled went like greased lightning." And he hadn't told her. Had he planned for her to shoot into the river? Chad's eyes were on the floor. "Did you mean for me to go into the river?"

"No, I thought you would stop first. Like before."

"So you could yell scaredy-cat at me?"

"No, I wasn't going to say anything." He picked up a book and seemed to be memorizing the title.

"You said it all those other times."

"That was different. You were being silly then."

"It wasn't different. Why do you hate me?"

He looked up, startled. "I don't."

"Then why are you always doing mean things to me?"

"I'm not."

"You're always throwing things at me, making faces at me, calling me names, tricking me. How would you like it if I did those things to you?"

He shrugged. "I wouldn't mind. That's how we play."

Abby didn't believe him. "You didn't like it when I threw a book at you and broke your house."

"That's because it was for the twins."

"You didn't like it when three of us threw snowballs at you."

"That's because it wasn't fair, three against one."

"It wasn't fair to throw snowballs in my face when I'd never even seen snow before."

"But it doesn't mean I hate you," Chad said. He blushed and kept his eyes on the foot of her bed, where McNab snuggled against her feet. "I, um, really guess I like you sort of."

Abby made a noise halfway between a laugh and a snort. "You like me! What would you do if you didn't like me?"

"Nothing, I guess. I haven't thought about it."

Chad didn't hate her. Abby could hardly believe it. Not only did he not hate her, he'd said he liked her. Sort of. She shook her head. It was too hard to believe.

"Do you hate me?" he asked.

Abby thought about it. "No. I just wish you were nicer sometimes. Most of the time."

"I could try."

Maybe he would. She'd probably have to remind him sometimes. Probably a lot of times. "It wasn't your fault I went into the river. I should've stopped sooner."

Chad looked out the window. "Yes, it was. You would've slowed down and stopped sooner if you'd known that the sled was going faster because of the waxed runners. You would've stopped no matter what names I called you."

"Maybe." Abby remembered how determined she had been to keep going so she wouldn't have to hear those dreaded words. What did it matter if he called her names? Falling through the ice was a lot worse than being called scaredy-cat. It was her fault for being so sensitive that she did something stupid, something she knew she shouldn't have done. "I shouldn't have let your teasing make me do something that scared me. It was only the second time I'd ever been on a sled. I should've slowed down."

"I'm sorry," he said. "I promise not to call you names anymore. Cross my heart." He crossed it and spat.

This was too much for Abby. Chad with his hair

combed, apologizing, promising not to tease her, crossing his heart, and spitting. "You better not say that. You know you will."

"No, I won't," he said. And then he grinned like the old Chad. "I'll try not to."

Abby grinned, too. "That's better."

"Want to play Monopoly?"

But the twins brought their Chinese checkers to cheer her up. Abby and Chad both groaned, but they all sat on her bed and played until the twins wanted to switch to another game they had just invented. They called it Snickerboffkins, and it involved dropping the marbles onto the checkerboard and tilting it until they fell into place.

"Um, I think we'll just watch you play," Chad said, raising an eyebrow at Abby.

She nodded. "Snickerboffkins looks too complicated."

"It's because you almost got drowneded," Polly said.

"And almost got frozed," Patty said. "Tomorrow you'll be warm enough."

"Then we can play Snickerboffkins all day," Polly said.

"I can hardly wait," Abby said as she and Chad exchanged looks.

Aunt Noreen brought Abby's supper on a tray and sent the twins and Chad downstairs for theirs. The tray held broth, plain toast, and a glass of grape juice. "I'll starve!" Abby protested. "Why can't I have left-overs?"

"Because you may be getting a fever," Aunt Noreen said. "Remember the old saying. Feed a cold and starve a fever."

"If you feed me real food, I'll be so strong that I won't get a fever," Abby coaxed.

Aunt Noreen smiled and shook her head. "Be a good patient now and eat your invalid food."

Abby nibbled the toast. She tried dunking it in the broth. It was like soggy cardboard. She broke it into lit-tle bits and put it in the bowl. McNab slurped it up and wagged his tail for more.

"Sorry, that's all. You were a good dog today. You tried to rescue me, too."

When her mother came to retrieve her tray, Abby complained that she was still hungry.

"Oh, Abby, if you're hungry, I know you're all right," she said with relief. "But I think you'd better not overload your stomach after such an ordeal."

My stomach is underloaded, Abby wanted to say. But it was no use arguing with a mother about such things. She would slip downstairs later. But she didn't have to. Chad smuggled her up a turkey sandwich and a chunk of fruitcake, which she devoured.

Chad seemed uncomfortable. He shifted around in

the chair several times while Abby ate. Finally he blurted, "I saw her."

"Who?" Abby licked fruitcake crumbs off her fingers.

"I saw the girl on the ice today. You weren't delirious. Unless I was, too."

"Why didn't you say so when they thought I was delirious?"

"They would think I was and I would be in bed, too. Who would bring us food then?"

He had a point.

"She was Felicia, wasn't she?"

Abby nodded. "I think so. What did you see?"

"A girl about your age wearing an old-fashioned red velvet dress and some kind of black buttoned boots. She had blonde hair. She reached into the water after you disappeared, and when you came up, she was holding your hand."

"She wouldn't let me go down again, even when I thought the water was warm and wanted to."

Chad raised his eyebrows in surprise. "That water must have been close to freezing. Why did you think it was warm?"

Abby shrugged. "I don't know. Your senses get sort of turned around. I thought you were trying to lasso me because you thought I was a cow."

"A cow!" He laughed. "I didn't think you were a cow. But you were awfully hard to lasso. A cow might have been easier. When you couldn't get your arm through the loop, Felicia put it in and guided you onto solid ice."

"What did you see then?" Abby asked.

"She disappeared. She was there and then she wasn't."

"That's how I remember it, too," Abby said.

"So I guess I've really seen a ghost."

"I guess you really have. You saw her before, too, that first night on the stairs."

"Yeah," he confessed, "I did. But I was too scared to admit it. Weren't you scared?"

"I was at first, but she was so sad I wasn't afraid of her. She seemed to be trying to tell me something. I didn't know what it was. But now I do. She was trying to warn me about the ice. I misunderstood.

"I've seen her every night," Abby went on. "And each time she got closer to me until she looked me straight in the eyes, and the last time she cried. I think she was sad and frustrated because she couldn't make me understand."

"Do you think she'll come back tonight?"

"I don't know. I hope so. I want to thank her. Do you want to come with me?"

"No." Chad shook his head emphatically. Some of his hair loosened from its combing and fell over his eyes. He looked more like his usual self.

"It's not scary," she told him.

But he wouldn't change his mind. "I'm glad she came back today and saved you. But seeing a ghost twice is enough."

Abby refrained from calling him 'fraidy-cat or scaredy-cat. She would wait until he called her names again, if he ever did, and then she would remind him that he was too scared to look at a ghost.

After he left, Abby started to read again until it was time to see Felicia, but she was tired from the cold and drifted off to sleep long before the downstairs clock struck nine.

EIGHTEEN

*A*bby awoke to a soft silence. Was it still Christmas night or already the next day? Something stirred at her feet.

McNab. She reached over and patted his head. "You're a good foot warmer, McNab."

He made a growly noise and showed his teeth in a grin. Abby's stomach made a growly noise and she got up. She put on her robe and slippers and looked out the window. It was barely daylight, and snow was falling hard. She had slept through the night and missed seeing Felicia.

"Come on, McNab. Let's go downstairs and get something to eat."

McNab hopped off the bed. He didn't need coaxing. He was always ready for food.

In the hall Abby looked for Felicia's footprints. The floor was dry. But if she'd come last night, her footprints would have dried up by now anyway. Maybe she hadn't come. Maybe she was allowed only one visitation per twenty-four hours. Maybe appearing in the daytime for a long period had used up all her ghostly energy.

In the kitchen Abby found a basket of leftover breads. She munched a wheat roll with a spoonful of Mrs. Elster's rhubarb jam. She gave McNab a roll to gnaw.

Uncle Thomas came downstairs in his robe. "Well, Abby, you look none the worse for your experience," he said cheerfully.

"I'm fine. I'm just hungry. You can take my temperature again, but I'm not eating any more of that invalid food."

He laughed. "That wasn't my doing, Abby. I'm all for my patients having anything they want to eat. But the nurses on the case overruled me."

Abby confessed what she had done, feeding it to McNab and eating what Chad had brought her. Uncle Thomas laughed louder. "Good for you."

Soon everyone was awake and the kitchen warmed with breakfast cooking.

"Looks like we're in for a day of snow," Aunt

Noreen commented as she spooned applesauce into a bowl.

Chad wanted to go outside to play in the falling snow, but the nurses refused to let any of them out. "You had enough of the cold yesterday," Aunt Noreen said. "A day in the house won't hurt you. Play with your Christmas presents."

The twins eagerly produced the Chinese checkers, but Abby and Chad both groaned "oh no" and said they couldn't play for another week at least.

The twins looked offended. "What's the matter with Chinese checkers?" Patty asked.

"What about Snickerboffkins?" Polly asked hopefully.

"Or Rugamuffalootin?" Patty asked.

Abby and Chad looked at each other and laughed.

The morning passed slowly after the excitement of Christmas. Abby snuggled into the parlor window seat to read. She finished another Nancy Drew and started *Eight Cousins*. Chad draped himself over the sofa and opened *Penrod and Sam*. Later she heard him snickering.

The snow fell steadily all morning, covering the ice on the river, hiding the place where Abby had fallen through. Was it snowing in Europe? It was probably already nighttime wherever her father was. Abby sat alone in the parlor after lunch and wondered if they would ever hear from him. He had been missing almost three months now, but it seemed like three years. She refused to think about him being killed. That wasn't possible.

Someone struggled through the deepening snow. His shoulders and cap were white with it. Uncle Thomas had said nobody would be out in this weather.

The man turned up the front walk, where the snow was over the tops of his boots. He was coming to their house. He wore a uniform under his overcoat. As he came closer, Abby realized he was a messenger from Western Union Telegraph, and her heart froze.

No! Go back! Don't come here! she wanted to shout.

Maybe nobody would hear him at the door. Maybe he would go away and later discover that he had made a mistake. He had almost gone to the wrong house to deliver a telegram, and wasn't it lucky nobody was home?

Abby kept quiet when she heard the knock on the door. What if this wasn't the wrong house? What if the news was about her father? Bad news? If they never answered the door, they would never have to know.

She covered her ears when the doorbell rang. She closed her eyes as Aunt Noreen hurried to answer. Time passed, but she didn't open her eyes or uncover her ears.

"Abby! Abby!"

Even with her ears covered, Abby heard her mother, but she didn't move. Her mother pulled Abby's hands away.

"Abby, what is the matter? We've had news of Daddy!"

"Is it bad?" Abby squinched her eyes tighter.

"He's alive, Abby. He's alive. He's a prisoner of war. Somewhere in Germany."

Abby opened her eyes. "Is that good?"

Mom hugged her. "He's alive, Abby. That's good. And he's out of the fighting. That's good. It's not good to be a POW, but he can survive. He can come back to us when this terrible war is over. Yes, it's good. It's very good. It's the best Christmas present I've ever had."

Abby couldn't help herself. She burst into tears. Then her mother cried, too, and at the same time, laughed. Aunt Noreen hurried in and hugged both of them, and she laughed and cried, and went to call Uncle Thomas.

"We have to celebrate," Uncle Thomas said.

"We'll have a party," Aunt Noreen said. She went to the telephone and invited all the neighbors over, Nancy and Ginny and Davy and their parents and others Abby hadn't met.

"What should I wear?" Abby asked her mother. The red velvet dress was ruined. Abby didn't think she ever wanted to wear a red velvet dress again. "I want to wear something Christmassy."

Chad offered his Christmas pullover. "It's not too big."

"What will you wear?"

"I have a dark green one."

Green was almost as festive as red. So Abby wore his red sweater with her old green corduroy skirt.

The neighbors came at six, bringing cookies, nuts, popcorn, and trays of deviled eggs, sliced meats, loaves of bread, and casseroles. Everyone hugged Abby and her mother, even the people she didn't know. McNab was in paradise, pouncing on dropped tidbits, snatching food from bowls left on the floor, lapping cocoa spilled in saucers.

When the grown-ups danced to Glenn Miller records, Davy asked Abby to dance. For Davy, that meant covering as much territory as possible. He galloped them all around the parlor, bumping into other couples, but they only laughed. Then it was Chad's turn. He was a better dancer than Davy, but Abby suspected he was counting under his breath.

The twins and Davy started a game of hide and seek.

"Do you want to dance or play?" Chad asked.

Abby sighed. She wanted to do both, and she suspected Chad did, too. "Let's play," she said, and they ran upstairs to join the game.

The company stayed until almost ten, walking home in the snow with their flashlights. Chad and Abby and the twins watched their progress from the parlor window, dark spots following light beams across the snow.

"It was a good party, wasn't it?" Mom said as they went upstairs together.

Abby nodded. "I wish Daddy had been here."

"We'll have another one when he comes home."

McNab made a nest on Abby's bed as she changed into pajamas and robe.

The house settled down for the night and gradually fell silent. Abby waited until the downstairs clock struck eleven. She slipped out of bed and tiptoed out of the room so McNab wouldn't wake up and insist on going with her.

The party spirit lingered in the parlor. Somebody had left a bowl under the Christmas tree. Two forgotten napkins lay crumpled on the window seat. A dish half full of salted nuts sat on the lamp table. A green ball had fallen from the Christmas tree. Abby hung it on a high branch just above the bluebird Mr. Elster had given her. She sat in the window seat to wait for Felicia and thought about the Stratton family living here eighty years ago. How terrible for William Stratton to survive the war and his wounds and then to return and find his daughter lost in the icy river. He probably never wanted to see the Stratton River again or any river with ice on it. Maybe that was why he moved his family to California, where it's sunny and warm.

Felicia, lost over the falls, stayed in New York, separated from her family. Abby hoped that she knew her father had survived the war. She was glad that her own father was safely away from the fighting and that she would be here when he returned from the war in Europe someday. Felicia hadn't come looking for her father or to be with a family but to warn Abby and then to save her from drowning in the river. It had been silly of Abby to think that wearing a red velvet dress could save her father. But it wasn't the dress's fault that she had fallen into the river. That might have happened anyway even if she had been wearing her hand-me-down snow clothes. The accident was her own fault for letting Chad's teasing get to her. Abby resolved not to let herself be bothered ever again by the names people called her.

The clock chimed the half hour. Where was Felicia? It was past the time she had always appeared before. Abby shivered and burrowed into the pillows on the window seat. The house was getting colder.

Maybe Felicia wasn't coming. Maybe she had used up all her appearances saving Abby from the river. Or maybe her mission was accomplished and she didn't have a reason to come back now—if ghosts had to have a reason for coming back and haunting a place. Reluctantly, Abby stood up to go back to her room.

"Thank you, Felicia," she whispered to the stillness of the parlor, hoping that wherever Felicia was, she could hear.

A current of warm air wafted over the room like a breath or a sigh, but Felicia didn't appear. Abby went into the hall. There on the slate floor, a set of wet footprints, growing ever fainter, led away from the parlor to the front door.